Readers are talking about Mia Kerick's Young Adult novels:

"Mia Kerick's writing is engaging and perfectly balanced."~ *Suki Fleet*

"One of the things I love the best about Ms. Kerick's writing is her ability to build a world where the characters feel real to me. I laugh with them and I cry with them. I rejoice and I mourn. It's a very special and gifted writer who can take their readers on a journey and make them feel like they're a part of it." ~ *Sandy*

"Mia's books should be made compulsory reading in high schools. She opens your eyes so wide to both sides of a story."
~ *Mandy Ryder*

"Mia Kerick has a way of taking an unusual or horrible situation and looking at it sideways." ~ *Lori*

"Author Mia Kerick is queen of the true love story in which the characters have to overcome internal issues to achieve it." ~ *Mtb*

"Kerick has full faith in the power of love to redeem the victimized and heal their wounds." ~ *Paula*

"In that way that Mia Kerick has, she gets right inside the characters heads and hearts and gives us the truth of them - not a cleaned up, perfect version." ~ *Lori*

"Mia Kerick has a way with teenage boys. They are all the same, and yet each one is unique. Straight or gay, they see the world with a combination of needy anxiety (which they fight not to express) and stubborn resistance (which they express readily). Writing YA novels about gay teens needs a delicate hand, and Kerick seems to have it."
~ *Ulysses Dietz*

"Mia Kerick is definitely going on my fave authors list for YA."
~ *Borderstar*

COME
TO MY
Window

Mia Kerick

To my mother and her fighting spirit.

1

"I'd do her, I know that much." Bart Pickler is gawking at the image on the inside wall of the subway car. "I mean, just look at her."

Believe me, I am. But I can't let that kinda trash talk just pass me by. "*Hello!* Female solidarity here—so cut the sleazy sex talk, Pickles." I make the universal gesture for "you've got a microscopic dick" with my thumb and forefinger and I look straight at his crotch.

"You just wish you *had* a pickle of your own, Justin Lara-Bieber!" Pickler snarls his retort with this irritating smile on his skinny lips, but it doesn't irk me too much. I've heard the *Justine Laraby/Justin Lara-Bieber* comparison probably a thousand times before. I'm basically immune to it. And yeah, I may wear my hair like Bieber did back in his "One Less Lonely Girl" days, and, sure, I look a lot like the dude, even without the hair, but that's where *most* of our similarities end.

"I think alls Pickles is saying here is that they definitely chose the right chick to slip her ass into a Lady Vixen costume, right Pickles?" Joey Fresco always tries to keep the peace.

Pickler and all the guys around me in the subway car nod—including a couple of guys who aren't even with our group. Like the rest of them, I study the wall panel. *Kemina: Nightingale Lingerie's Baby Vixen.*

Seriously, man—*Baby Vixen*? Sounds like a name for a kiddie porn star. But there she is—the *usually* hollow-eyed girl I see when I look out my bedroom window and across the alley—in all of her slutty-fox-costumed glory. And her eyes don't look at all hollow in this poster. In fact, Kemina has a very naughty and filled-with-even-naughtier-promises—but somehow still innocent—look in her eyes that I never see when she holds up a sign and gazes at me across the distance of fifteen feet.

So why am I looking at the *eyes* of the girl on this hot poster that's designed to inspire me, another teenage girl, to want my very own matching bra and undies set from The Nightingale Lingerie Shoppe? There's so much more to see... mile-long legs and a tiny waist and all of that smooth brown skin decorated with tiny, sexy scraps of green lace. But the lies in Kemina's dark eyes just keep pulling my attention right back up.

"She's just another girl," I say out loud like I couldn't give a shit, and then I grab my Red Sox cap off the bench beside me, stick it on my head, and pull it low over my eyes.

Pickles ain't gonna let that slide. "And Big Papi's just another DH." David Ortiz is my baseball hero, and these guys all know about my obsession with him.

"Nap time," I tell them with a yawn. "Wake me up when it gets good, and if it doesn't get good, wake me up when we get to the Y."

I hang with these guys so much that I frequently find myself wallowing in the "git 'er done" sex gutter right along beside them. But I can't jump into the gutter with these guys when it comes to Kemina. No matter how much I might want to, I can't.

2

This little peeking-at-each-other-through-the-window game has been going on for a hella long time now. Maybe it's been too long for *my* mental health, but I hang onto the hope that it hasn't yet lasted long enough. The thing is, lately it hasn't seemed so much like a game as it did in the beginning. Cuz the look in her eyes over the past couple days tells me this has turned into something much more like serious business. As if maybe I'm some kinda lifeline.

Tonight she's doing sit-ups. I hold the sit-ups record at my high school, but I'd say she's blowing me away. I'm not exactly counting, but if I had to guess, I'd say that she's done maybe a couple hundred. So, yeah, I'm impressed cuz that shit ain't easy to pull off. And I'm also a little bit worried, cuz she isn't what you'd call the girl-jock type. Not by a long shot.

I grab my sketchbook and open to an empty page.

How many sit-ups?

Like always, I write with my royal blue Sharpie, and press it to the wide picture window in my bedroom.

In the matching brownstone on the other side of the narrow alley, she moves to the center of *her* bedroom's picture window, which is directly across from mine. With a flowered hand towel, she wipes her forehead, and then her flat belly that's gotten a bit damp with sweat. And she shrugs. I can see her ribs poking out beneath her cut-off T-shirt.

I write again and then hold up another sign.

You did a lot—like maybe hundreds.

Her hair is long and silky and dark. I *think* I read somewhere that she's Hispanic, but I *know* she's the prettiest girl I've ever seen. I'd actually call her perfect. She tugs on the elastic that holds her hair in a high ponytail and the way her back arches as she does it is just so… so freaking awesome. That beautiful silky hair falls down all over her bony shoulders, and keeps on falling 'til it's nearly covering up her sort of sunken in chest—the sight of which makes me think about family shit I'd much rather forget. Then she shrugs again and that kinda brings me back to earth.

Kemina Lopez stands there and stares across the alley at me, her hollow dark eyes fixed on my face. She's not smiling, but not really frowning either; what I notice most is her total lack of expression. And she has no idea that my name is Justine Laraby. But I know her name—everybody does. And though there's nothing plain about her, we all know her as just plain "Kemina"—no last name necessary.

Cuz the girl across the narrow alley is the only Kemina that matters to us.

To me.

3

Basketball at the Y tonight wore me out. And then when I finally got home, Dad was out with Pam, so me and my bros made grilled cheese and tomato sandwiches for dinner. Now I'm upstairs in my room, sitting at my desk, getting ready to force myself to study. It's just so hard for me to buckle down and get my ass in gear, though. Always has been. I'm the polar opposite of a nerd.

I tell myself I'm not gonna peek into Kemina's bedroom tonight, but I pretty much immediately disobey my own orders. Sticking my chin in my hand, and then my elbow on the desk, I turn super casually toward the window. Her curtains are drawn about two thirds of the way, but I can still see inside her room pretty well.

Tonight her mom's in there with her. Kemina's mom is like a short and much more scary-looking, older version of Kemina. I know it's bullshit to label people cuz Dad drills that into me and my brothers' heads on a daily basis, plus I've personally been on the wrong end of that labeling shit. But the truth is, Kemina's mom seems like a total bitch. And I can't even hear what she's saying.

Very slowly and with great nonchalance, I turn my whole body toward the window. I think to grab *To Kill a Mockingbird* from off my desk and stick it on my lap in case I need to disguise my peeping-Tom-like behavior. And I watch. It's not as creepy as it sounds—Kemina watches me a lot too.

It's one of those clothes-trying-on nights. On these nights, Kemina's mother sits on the edge of her bed, kind of upright/uptight with her back all stiff and her legs crossed primly, and she observes as Kemina tries on clothes. And more clothes. And then some more. Usually these clothes-trying-on sessions go on for hours, until Kemina is red in the face and sweating her ass off.

Underneath all of the outfits she puts on, Kemina wears a sports bra and tiny bootie shorts so she never gets completely naked, or anything, and I'm not seeing more than I see when she exercises. This is how I excuse myself for my spying.

She tries on all kinds of stuff. Being a jeans and T-shirt sort of person, I'm not into the heights of fashion, but I still know what looks good on a girl when I see it. First Kemina tries on jeans, and lots of 'em. Some of them I've seen before, and some seem new, but they all make her butt look stellar. And after the jeans, she starts with the dresses. And some short skirts. And clingy tops, too.

I try to read my book, and I actually do, a little bit, but it's impossible to keep my mind on a book when she finally tries on one of her Vixen costumes. Since about October—I figure it must've been when she turned eighteen—Kemina has been Nightingale Lingerie's "Vicious Green Vixen". On the runway— I know this cuz I've seen clips on those cheesy late-night entertainment shows on TV, as well as in commercials and magazine ads—she always wears green. Not too much fabric covers her girl parts, but what little is there is forest green. Right now she's rocking a tiny green strapless nighty with this ivy- looking stuff kinda growing all over it. Can't help it—my eyes are glued to her ass as she bends down and pulls on these thigh high black boots.

This is when things get what I'd call disturbing. After she zips her boots, her mother beckons and Kemina walks over to the bed, and when she gets there her mom pushes her so she'll turn around. Then her mom lifts the skirt of the little green dress-thing, grabs a hold of Kemina's right butt cheek, and pinches. When Kemina pulls away, her mother says something that makes Kemina's pretty face get all wrinkled up and she looks like she's gonna cry. My hands ball up into fists and I'm pretty sure I called it right—Kemina's mom is a total bitch.

Something is just *so* not right over there. I'm so pissed, I kind of involuntarily stand up, and the movement gets "Bitchy Mom's" attention. Right after Kemina's mother and I catch eyes, Mom gets up off the bed, steps to the window, and pulls the curtains closed. So, the peep show is over and I'm left to wonder about why the lady pinched her daughter's ass and what she said right after she pinched it. And I wonder how Kemina is doing right now.

But I think I kind of know what's up.

"Bitchy Mom" told Kemina she's getting fat, or some crock of shit like that.

It pisses me off, but what am I supposed to do?

4

I'm not on the girls' basketball team at my school cuz it's lame. No offense, and I'm *not* saying that *all* girls' teams are lame. It's just that *my* all-girls private school, Upper West Side Achievement Academy is not known for its athletics. I'm also aware that this is a pretty abysmal way to make decisions about which sports I'm gonna play at school, but I can't forget that when I was just a freshman and I made girls varsity basketball, I kept stomping on the other girls on the opposing team as well as my own team—and hard. They got injured and I was frustrated by the whole experience. So now I meet up at least a couple of times a week after school with my guy friends from the neighborhood and we play streetball until the weather gets too cold and the outdoor courts are covered in snow, and then we switch over and play at the YMCA in a pickup league until the snow melts.

At first the YMCA directors didn't want a girl to play in the boys' league, but then they caught a load of me in action and changed their minds.

Right now I sit at Naldo's Café on Broadway waiting for the guys. The thing that sucks is that I have to wait 'til their high school team after-school practices are over *and* 'til they get all the way over here to go to the Y and play with them. So we can only play for a little while cuz they've got homework, which I got mostly done while waiting for them. And on game days, I try to go and support their teams as much as I can, so there's no basketball on those days either. I can't wait for spring when the regular season is over so we can hit the street and play pickup. On a brighter note, though, softball at Upper West Side Achievement Academy doesn't completely suck so I'm on the varsity girls' softball team. But I can hit anything any of the pitchers in the league hurl my way, which is kind of a good and bad thing at the same time.

I sit there in the back of the deli with just an energy drink on the table in front of me. "I'm totally starving," I mumble to myself, get up, and push my chair in. Reaching into the side leg pocket of my skinny cargo pocket khakis—the school uniform is a khaki skirt and white button-down but they bend the rules so I can wear pants instead—I pull out a couple of bills and head for the bakery area. One of those oversize chocolate chip cookies they make here will get me through b-ball until dinnertime. I saunter over to the café area and lean against the glass counter in front of me.

And that's when I see her.

Kemina's dark glasses, gray beanie, and long black overcoat do nothing to disguise her. Nearly six feet tall, unruly black hair tossed without a plan all over her shoulders, and those puffed-up lips—well, I couldn't miss her if I tried.

I think she sees me too, but it's hard to tell with the sunglasses.

"She leans toward the cash register. "Large black decaf." Her voice is deep and raspy. I'm completely caught up in her.

"That'll be three dollars."

Kemina pulls a fiver out of her overcoat pocket. I look at her hands. Long fingers, much paler than I expected based on the skin tone of her face. "Keep it." As she waits for her coffee, she very gradually turns toward me. For some reason, I run my hands though my shaggy hair as if I'm nervous. Maybe I *am* nervous. I want to say hello, and my lips even shape the word, but no sound comes out from between them.

"What'll it be, son?" The server's voice breaks me out of my love spell. I know that I'm the "son" he is talking to, as I'm always getting confused for a boy. Usually I like it that way. Right now I'm not so sure.

"Um...." I want to order my usual *Chocolate Chunk Extreme* cookie but it sounds so undignified compared to a *large black decaf.* "How about one of those?" I point to the cookie through the glass.

"A *Chocolate Chunk Extreme* or *Cinnamon Snickerdoodle to the Max*?"

I should have known I wouldn't get through this moment unscathed. "One of th-those chocolate chip ones," I stutter.

I *think* Kemina is still watching me, although the shades don't let me know for sure. As a matter of fact, she's so wrapped up in either me, or the sight of the cookie I'm ordering, that she doesn't notice *her* server as she hands her the cup of coffee.

"Your coffee, ma'am."

"Uh...oh, thank you." She grabs the cup and, without hesitation, turns around. As I wait for my *Chocolate Chunk Extreme* cookie, I glance at the door to watch Kemina leave. And with the hand that isn't holding the coffee, she lowers her sunglasses and our eyes meet.

They are as cold and dark and hollow as I remember from the window the other night.

I wonder what she sees in my eyes when she looks at me.

5

My younger twin bros are hanging out with me in my room tonight. Dad's gone again—it seems that dating a high maintenance lady takes a lot of his time and energy—so we're eating the calzones we ordered from the Italian place on the next block up here in my third floor bedroom.

"Eat over your paper plates, and no wiping your grimy fingers on my rug," I tell Jake and Jory who are sitting on the floor beside my bed.

"Awesome—so you sayin' we can wipe 'em on your Oklahoma Thunder bedspread?"

I look straight at Jake, AKA, the jazzed-bro, from my place on said bedspread, and I grin. "Funny, Jake. Try it and see what happens."

He laughs and replies, "I'm too young to die."

Jory looks pissed-off, which isn't unusual for him. I call him the emo-bro for good reason. And he was a little bit that way before Ma left, so I can't blame this one all on her.

"Wha's up, Emo? Something wrong with your calzone? I told you not to get both grilled chicken *and* meatballs in the same one." I wrinkle my nose, even though it doesn't sound half-bad.

"My calzone doesn't suck." That translates into "it's pretty good." And it also means I'm supposed to play twenty questions about what's got him in his current funk.

"Bad grade on that science quiz?"

He shakes his head and rips off a good size corner chunk of his calzone with his side teeth. "Aced it."

"Cat piss in your back pack again?" Big Papi the cat is getting old and he does that kind of shit every now and then.

He *almost* finishes chewing and answers. "Better not have."

"Jory's pissed that Dad's out with Pamela Perkins again," Jake informs me.

Pamela Perkins. Perky Pamela Perkins. Precious Proper Perplexing Pam.

"I guess he's into her," I offer blandly. There's no accounting for taste, and Dad has been alone for a long time, so....

"She's a bitch." Jory knows we aren't supposed to refer to people that way, but I'm guilty of the same crime so I don't correct him. Hypocrites are the world's lowest life form.

"I don't think she's *that* bad." Jake is eyeing my OKC Thunder bedspread, and his greasy fingers are twitching like he wants to smear them on it. "She cooks sometimes."

Yes, food is the way to my jazzed-bro's heart, and we're like the royal family of takeout, grilled cheese sandwiches, and frozen meals, so anybody who cooks real food for Jake is okay in his book.

"She makes us wait to eat 'til after them two finish," Jory reminds us.

True, that. We're second-class citizens, at least at this point, when Precious Pam comes over, but I'm hoping that once Dad "gets some" he'll find his backbone and inform her that we three kids are an important part of his life.

"Maybe if we cook them dinner and set the table for five she'll get the idea," I suggest weakly.

"That he's our dad and she can't have him?" Yup. Jory's pissed.

"That she can't have him all to herself." Jake seems to pick up on the finer points of subtle suggestion quicker than Jory. "Whatcha' gonna cook, Jussy?"

"Nothing if you guys don't throw away all of your trash and go do your homework—like pronto." Now *Jake* looks a little bit emo, so I answer his question. "How about I make spaghetti casserole? You like that, right?"

"With garlic bread?"

"Better." I wink at him. "Cheesy garlic bread."

He's easy. Wearing this giant grin, Jake starts wrapping up his trash into a ball. But Jory tilts his head and I know he's going to ask me a tough one. "You gonna be the one to invite her?"

"Sure." *What choice do I have?* "I'll ask her for Sunday afternoon, 'kay?"

Jory gets up slowly and folds his arms as if he's gonna leave his trash scattered on the floor of my bedroom. "She's prob'ly gonna say no."

"Well, we won't know 'til we give it a shot."

Emo-bro nods once and then bends over and picks up his trash. "Good luck, Jussy. You're gonna need it." Wrappers in hand, he leaves my bedroom.

I pick up my own trash and toss it into my Knicks trash barrel. As I do, I glance over to try and make eye contact with Kemina cuz she was staring in my room, off and on, the whole time my bros were in here. The expression in her eyes looks different tonight—it's kinda a longing look. She's probably in the mood for a large meatball parmesan calzone with extra sauce just like I was.

She takes her notebook and writes something on it with a black marker. Then she gets up and comes to the window. The marker she uses tonight has a finer tip than usual, so it's kinda hard to read.

Are those your little brothers?

I nod. Then I write on my sketchpad in my usual royal blue.

Jake and Jory. Twins. 7th grade. Jory is the one who looks pissed-off. Jake looks stoked.

Kemina reads it, and then smiles. She is so pretty when she smiles that I get goose bumps up my arms. She leans down to write in her notebook again.

What's your name?

I thought you'd never ask. ☺ *Justine Laraby. Pleased to officially meet you.* We've been peeking at each other across the alley for months.

I'm Kemina Lopez.

Am I supposed to act like that's news to me? I decide to just tell her the truth.

I noticed. ☺

Kemina smiles again, and her eyes take on a look I don't think I've ever seen since we've "met" or, in other words, since we started exchanging messages through our windows. It's kinda a more animated look than usual, but not in that sexy, I'm-going-to-make-you-feel-so-good-when-I-get-you-alone, kind of way. Like the Vixen on the poster in that subway car suggests.

It's nothing like that. She just looks more or less happy.

Kemina, I write, *want to meet me at Naldo's Café, where we saw each other today?*

It takes a lot of balls, so to speak, to press that last sign up against the window, but I do it.

She pulls her hair up off her shoulders, and then lets it all spill down through her fingers like a silky black waterfall, and I so badly want to touch it. I have a feeling I'm not the only person out there who would get off on doing that, though. She nods, and writes.

When?

How about tomorrow after school? Like at three?

She nods again.

I scribble something and hold the sign up to the window.

Let's do our homework together tonight.

Kemina tilts her head, clearly confused.

You got tunes?

She nods one more time.

Got any Alanis Morissette?

I just have a feeling about this. This time I get a smile.

Put it on and I will too. Then sit on your bed, and I'll sit on mine. And we can do our homework together.

The smile I get from her is stunning, and I'm not joking when I say it steals my breath away. She grabs her notebook and writes.

Why not?

And so I shrug, cuz I can't think of a reason why we shouldn't do this.

But I can't help but wonder who Kemina thinks about when Alanis Morissette sings those lyrics of accusatory blame in "You Oughta Know".

6

I know what the meaning of the word surreal is when I join
Kemina at a table for two in the back of Naldo's Café. I sincerely
wish I knew its meaning on Tuesday when I took my vocabulary
quiz, but, oh, well. I never stress too much about grades.
Generally speaking, I do okay at school without putting forth an
extraordinary effort. But I *do* have a new understanding of the
word surreal right now.

She's drinking a cup of tea—just a small one—which makes
me wonder if she doesn't plan on staying too long. I slide into the
seat across from her and drop my basketball on an empty chair at
the next table over, and then stick my plastic bottle of chocolate
milk on the table between us.

"Hey." Not exactly a moment of conversational genius on my
part, but whatever—cuz she looks up at me. *And* she takes off her

shades, so I figure that the hardest part is done. "You're early, Kemina, seeing as I'm pretty sure I'm not late." I make an effort to deepen my voice cuz I feel more confident when I sound more like a guy—don't know why. I've tried to figure it out about ten thousand times, but I can never find a real concrete reason.

"Kemi. You can call me Kemi." Her voice is breath-filled and sultry, but she looks at me with that hollow gaze that doesn't match her words *or* her tone.

And Kemi's wearing all black again, just like when I saw her here yesterday. She must think that the black clothing helps to hide her but it really doesn't. Her beauty is what I'd call astonishing. Loose dark clothing can't begin to disguise that shit. I get up and head around the table to stand beside her.

"Let me help you with your coat." First of all, I want to establish that although I'm also a girl, I didn't meet her here in an effort to be her BFF. I want to be her date—the one she thinks of *like that.* And secondly, I want her to take off her coat and stay a while. Two birds, one stone. Now if I can just get her out of that long black overcoat.

She looks up at me with hesitance, tilts her head like she's thinking about it, and then stands and allows me to pull her coat off of her shoulders. I can't help it. I think, *Score!*

Before I sit back down, I ask, "You hungry? Cuz they're heating me up a couple of slices of deep-dish cheese pizza. I'm about to go pick it up at the counter by the pizza oven, but I can get you something else if you'd rather."

Kemina shakes her head. "No, thank you. I'm fine."

When I come back, I put one slice of pizza in front of her and one in front of me, and then I sit back down across from her. "So, Kemi," I try out the nickname and it feels good rolling off my tongue, "it's kind of weird to see you without glass between us. It's like we're zoo animals that cut loose from our glass cages and…came to a café."

Double-score! She smiles, and this time I can see teeth. Quickly, though she hides her mouth behind her cup of tea.

"So, Kemi, where do you go to school?" I figure it must be some private school for actors and entertainers, or something.

"In my bedroom." She lowers her head but lifts her eyes to look at me. I'd thought she had dark eyes, but I realized I'd been mistaken. I mean, her eyebrows are dark, and her eyelashes too—but her eyes are a deep green, like a shamrock. *Jeez.*

"There's a high school in your bedroom?" Um, I don't think so. "You have tutors come over, or something like that?" I'd never seen anyone besides Kemina and her mother in her bedroom.

"No. I'm enrolled in an online secondary school program. I'm due to finish high school classes in a couple of weeks."

"You got an early graduation date?"

"No. It's not really early—classes are done at your own individual pace, and I got ahead of pace this summer."

Well, this is stimulating conversation. School talk... way to hook her in. I try to shift our focus. "Nice...um, tights." I am lame; it's a fact. "I like the printy-pattern thing they got going on."

"Thanks. They're nothing special. I stole them from a job, I think."

She brought it up, not me. "Like a modeling job? You *stole* them?"

Kemina crosses her legs. "It's not really stealing, J-Justine." I can tell she is trying out my name too. "We can take what we want after we wear it for a shoot. At least I could when I worked for Jonas and Judas Juniors Jeans. It's different now that I'm doing Nightingale stuff and swimsuits for other lines."

"Yeah." Yeah, I am clearly out of my league in the fashion arena. "You play any sports?" *Like, duh!* She is schooled online—there are no *online* high school sports teams.

But luck is with me, cuz she doesn't seem to think the question is stupid at all. "Not so much on teams, but I work out a lot."

"Like all the sit-ups and push-ups you do in your room?" I think of her bedroom, all pastel colors and flowery patterns and I just bet it smells like a meadow, too, even when she sweats.

Kemina nods, "I also spin at a gym in Midtown."

"Cool."

"And you play basketball?"

"What gave it away?" We both look over at my well-used basketball resting in the chair beside me. I want to pat myself on the back cuz I got her to smile at me again and I wonder how many more smiles I can get out of her this afternoon. So I push the slice at her. "Go for it. Have your pizza—don't be shy, Kemi."

"No, I really can't." She sips her tea. "But it sure smells good."

"Well, that's your slice. Don't expect me to be eating it for you." I lift my piece to my lips and take a bite. "It tastes as good as it smells. In case you were wondering." I just finish thinking that things are going swell, when everything changes.

There's a flash in my face and next thing I know it, Kemina is sticking her dark glasses back on her perfect nose. "Put your hood up." She says it in a low voice, and as I do she grasps her coat and pulls it on. It's wrapped tightly around her in a split second. "No pictures," she growls, and holds up her hand in front of this big camera that has seemingly joined our intimate party of two.

"Is this guy your boyfriend, Kemina?" The dude who's holding the camera, a real Clark Kent-looking type, asks as if he has a right to the information. "What's his name?"

"Leave us alone!" Kemina's pissed. "Jesus, can't I even have pizza with a friend without you guys getting all up in my face?" That soft and sultry sound of Kemina's voice is history. She's irate, and she doesn't care if we all know it. "Now take a frigging hike."

I can already see that there's no way this guy is going anywhere. He's already dropped his backpack and is leaning against the wall. The camera flashes a few more times. So I stand up and then help Kemi to her feet. "Let's get out of here."

The photographer gets right in my face. "What's your name?"

I shrug and say, "Justin Bieber." And then Kemina and I head for the door.

7

"Hi Pam." Tonight I got home too late to order food and wait for delivery cuz I went and played basketball with the guys *after* I walked Kemina home, so it looks like it's is gonna be another PB&J night for the boys and me. "Where's Dad?"

"He went upstairs to settle a minor dispute between the boys." Sitting behind me at the kitchen table, I don't miss that she looks really pretty. Strawberry-hair, toffee-colored eyes, evenly freckled face—adorable human female version of a cocker spaniel kind of pretty. Like Lindsey Lohan if she hadn't gone down the wrong path. Not the kind of pretty I'm into, but to each his, or her, own. "Do these types of peacemaking excursions usually take very long?"

I turn away from the sticky counter and look back at her with raised eyebrows. "Settling disputes between the twins can take all night." I bite my lip, as if I'm really sorry to tell her that.

And once again, I think it's my lucky day, cuz Precious Pam buys my little fabrication. She stands up and pushes in her chair all the way, because it's the right thing to do. "Well, I have to be at the office early tomorrow." She looks from her watch to the wrought iron rooster-shaped clock on the wall, which my friends refer to as the wrought iron cock clock, but I choose not to share that tidbit of information with my father's oh-so-proper girlfriend who is really *nothing at all* like Lindsey Lohan. "Would you do me a little favor, doll?"

She always calls me *doll*. That word alone, without the sing-song quality of Pam's voice, makes me cringe. Dolls are creepy. I never played with them—my only exposure to dolls was through horror movies, where they grinned evilly before snapping somebody's neck.

"At your service, Pam." I turn back around to slice the six sandwiches, one after another. I figure six sandwiches should fill the three of us. Dad's on his own for dinner, as far as I'm concerned.

"Would you tell your Daddy that his *Pamewah* had to go home to get her *booty sweep*?"

I fight the urge to vomit, and I nod.

Really, Dad? What're you thinking? Are you this horny? Or is it that you're just sick of being lonely?

"You have to say it *just like that*, doll." Pam steps over to me, reaches up cuz I'm about a foot taller than her, and turns me around kinda roughly by the shoulders. The look in her eyes tells me that this is serious business. She repeats what I'm supposed to tell Dad, but more slowly this time. "Pamewah. Had. To. Go. Home. To. Get. Her. Booty. Sweep."

"Got it." I have a feeling if I don't change the subject soon she's gonna make me practice saying it out loud. And that's about dead last on the list of things I want to do tonight. "By the way, Pam, the boys were wondering if you might want to come over for a late lunch on Sunday afternoon. Us three'll cook."

She wrinkles her button nose. It's a cute little nose, I'm not gonna lie, but all wrinkled up as it is right now, as if she's disgusted at the prospect of Jake and Jory and me touching her food, causes one word to echo in my head. And that one word starts with a B, and ends with an itch. I mean, it's not like the idea of the twins' grimy fingers poking at *my* food doesn't totally gross me out too, but I don't wrinkle my nose like that. Precious Pamela Perkins needs to make more of an effort when it comes to Jake and Jory. I personally couldn't give a shit about how she treats me.

In her ladylike pumps, she strides evenly down the hall and to the door.

"Don't let the door hit you in your perky ass on your way out!" I call—NOT! But I want to pretty badly.

I pass Dad on the stairs as I carry the paper plates with the not-so-gourmet sandwiches on them and an eight pack of red Gatorade hanging from my pinky, which I'll admit kinda hurts. "You left Pamela all alone in the kitchen?" He looks mildly concerned.

"She took off." I'm honestly a little bit pissed at him for ditching us so often lately, mostly cuz it messes with Jory's head. "Easy *come*, easy go." I'm not sure why I add that.

"What's that supposed to mean, Jussy?" He stops me by nudging my side with his elbow and then he unhooks the Gatorade from my straining pinky.

"What do you *think* it means?" Somebody needs to teach the dude how to be a better dad. And it looks like I'm the only candidate available.

Dad shakes his head. "Yeah…I know. I've been less than Father of the Year lately. Got all wrapped up in—"

"Pamewah's booty." Not to sound sarcastic, but so what. "Side note, Dad: she wants you to know that she's home resting it right now."

Dad has the good grace to blush. There's no getting around it—emo-bro, jazzed-bro, and me are this guy's kids. We look like a clan of Justin Bieber clones. Fair skin, light brown hair that cooperates with about any hairstyle we try, slightly angelic looking faces with a devil's expression in our brown eyes. Although last year I saw on YouTube that his eye color changes with his moods, thanks to colored contact lenses. When you look so much like Justin Bieber, you need to keep up with all Bieber-related gossip.

"Ya got me there, which is rather, um, TMI, isn't it?" He calls the boys. "Jake, Jory—family meeting on the stairs!"

My dad's the spontaneous type, about which Pamela shudders and accuses him of living life by the seat of his pants. And Dad drops onto the seat of his pants now, right here on the stairs, and so I follow suit. "Is one of these for me?" He asks, glancing at the plates.

I nod, which is a lie, but I can live with one PB&J instead of two. And Dad looks so guilty—I decide that the man in front of me is the picture of what Justin Bieber will look like at forty, when he's in the doghouse. And unless the real Bieber turns his act around, the doghouse is where he's heading. Just saying.

The boys scramble halfway down the stairs to where we sit. "Stairs-picnic," Dad announces, and he rips a couple of Gatorades off the eight-pack and hands them to the boys. We proceed to have a rather odd family dinner, chatting on the dusty staircase over paper plates and thrown together sandwiches.

"Sorry I've been among the missing so much lately," Dad says when our plates are empty and the boys' sticky fingers have been licked clean—by the boys, not by Dad and me. *Yuck.* "Pam and I should try to spend more time with you guys."

Jake and Jory look at me in unison.

"Well, since you brought it up, Dad, I invited Pam to have lunch with us on Sunday."

"You did?" Dad looks a little bit worried. "And she said?"

"No official verbal answer. All I got from her was a wrinkled nose."

Dad nods, and I am certain he is quite familiar with Pam's crinkled-up nose look.

"But I'm gonna take it as a yes." I reach all around and pick up the empty plates. "Three o'clock on Sunday. Spaghetti casserole. You get a nice loaf of Italian bread, Dad. I'm gonna make the garlic bread that Jake likes. And don't forget a couple of bottles of whatever wine Pam is into." I'm pretty sure she's gonna need it.

"Cool," Dad says, taking the trash from me. "I'll grab a pie or something for dessert, too."

"Whoopie pies." Jory says it with deadly seriousness. If I were Dad, I'd get the boy some Whoopie pies.

"Your wish is my command, Prince Jory." Dad stands and bows very formally.

Jory finally cracks a grin and it's really good to see. It's been a while.

"In that case, get some black and white cookies, too." Jake doesn't miss a trick.

Having our family meal on the stairs was kinda cozy, but I will say I'm happy to be back up in my room. Trying to be casual, I flop onto my bed, look through my wide window into Kemina's room, and I notice that although the curtains are pulled, I can still see through them a little bit. These are new curtains, I realize, a lighter color peach than before, the flower print kind of built right into the sort of sheer fabric. I can see her shape walking around behind them. And then she comes to the center of her window and pushes the new curtains open. It's as if the sun has burst through the clouds.

Kemina is so beautiful, more so, now, since we met in person. It's like something is real between us that was merely a fantasy before. She presses a loose piece of yellow construction paper, on which she has already written a note in black marker, against the window.

Sorry about the paparazzi.

I grab my sketchpad and scribble down my response. Then I get up off my bed and go to my window to show it to her.

Must admit, it was a first for me. Do you think they'll figure out I'm not a dude?

She tilts her head, and seems to think about that for a minute. Then she takes her marker from the windowsill and writes on the bottom of the yellow paper.

If they see us together in public again, they'll make a point of finding out exactly who you are. Is it worth it to you?

I've never before had an official reason to come out of the closet. I've long figured that the world, in general, just assumes I'm gay for all of the typical, or maybe stereotypical, reasons.

To start with, I dress like a dude. Before I started at Upper West Side Achievement Academy (UWSAA) Dad went in to see the principal to get permission for me to wear pants instead of a skirt, which is their uniform, to school. He had to spell it out for them: Justine wears pants or we find another private school. Lo and behold—Justine was allowed to wear pants. What nobody knew until physical education class when we had to change into gym uniforms, though, was that underneath those pants I wore boxer briefs. White button-down-collar shirts are the required shirts at UWSAA, which does not pose a problem for me. Before I put it on, though, I strap on the tightest sports bra I can find to press in what little Mother Nature endowed me with. Then I throw on a white V-neck T-shirt to hide the bra, and on top of that, a white button-down-collar oxford shirt from the men's department at Ralph Lauren, a size large, which I swim in. When I'm not at school, it's jeans and a T-shirt, or basketball attire. Then there are my beloved oversized gray sweats, which I live in at home. High tops are the norm—and I'm something of a sneaker collector so there's no shortage for me to pick from—and on mega-dress-up-days, there are always boat shoes. And I'm not above wearing rugged black combat boots, unlaced and badass looking. But all in all, except for the shoes, I'm an uncomplicated sort.

Then there's the boy's haircut and the lack of any makeup whatsoever. I've never had my ears pierced, but I *do* sport a tiny nose ring on my right nostril. My nails have never been painted, well, except for my left index finger that got painted a bright fuchsia at Lani Currier's birthday party back in first grade. All it took was for Lani to paint *one* of my fingernails and I got upset. Okay, maybe I went totally ballistic, so Lani's mother quickly rubbed the polish off my fingernail onto a paper towel. But I was so freaked out that Dad had to come and get me. That was my last girly-girl slumber party. I don't bond well with the uber-feminine, I guess.

Beyond appearances, I'm really athletic, in general, and, not to brag, but I'm the star of the varsity softball team, in specific. Outside of school, I hang with mainly guys I went to grade school with cuz we like to do the same shit, and in school, I hang with the girl-jocks. I have an Oklahoma City Thunder comforter, a plain navy blue rug on my bedroom floor, and a cat named Big Papi.

And the day I turn eighteen, I'm getting a tattoo. I've been itching for a Boston Red Sox B with the number 34 for David Ortiz beside it on my right hip—*not* to be confused with a tramp stamp.

Do these things make me gay? I don't think so. Maybe they make the way I express my gender kinda masculine, but that doesn't mean I'm gay. And contrary to popular belief, it doesn't mean I wanna be a guy. I really think when it comes to gender it's a wide spectrum and human beings fall here and there, all over it. In a nutshell—I'm a girl; I want to continue being a girl, but I also like girls. I don't see that status changing. At least not in this lifetime.

So I shrug and write on the next blank piece of paper in my sketchbook.

I have nothing to hide.

By the way I look at her, I try to imply *do you?* But Kemina either doesn't pick up on it, or she isn't willing to answer. I'm not exactly in the position to make harsh demands on the girl to come out of the closet, so I accept her silence. Then she flips over the yellow paper, presses it against the window, and writes something very quickly.

I like you, Justine.

I start to gesture that I feel the same way, but she's already writing again.

Let's push our beds up against the windows. Then we can see each other better when we study.

I nod, and we both immediately go to work on moving our beds. Neither of us have big beds with heavy frames. We're both still sleeping in our "kid-decorated" bedrooms, in twin-sized beds. It only takes a minute and they are pressed against the windows. If the alley wasn't between us we'd be sleeping together. *Damned alley*, I think and smile. It feels like a wicked smile, and I may have waggled my eyebrows very slightly, but nobody can prove that. I cover my mouth with my hand, but I think it's too late, and she saw me leering. *My bad.*

Kemina's eyes light up with laughter. She sits down at the foot of her bed, grabs the yellow paper, and, pressing it against her thigh, starts to write, but is interrupted when her mother storms into her bedroom. And the woman is PO'd. Kemina stuffs the yellow paper between her bed and the wall, from what I can see, and she snaps to attention like her mother is a drill sergeant. For Mrs. Lopez's—I assume that's her name—benefit, I get up and act as if I'm leaving the room, even going so far as to turn off the light, but I linger in the doorway where they can't see me, and I watch.

First her mother points to the bed and then her right ear and makes a gesture indicating major irritation, complete with an eye roll. She seems to be complaining about the racket Kemina made when moving her bed. I also notice she's carrying something in her left hand, but I can't tell what it is. All I can see is that it's square and metal. She places it on the floor and then stands back up and points to it. When Kemina steps up, I know it's a scale. They both look down at its verdict.

Mrs. Lopez's head is lowered as she shakes it back and forth. Kemina just stands there, still on the scale, and still staring down. Finally she steps off. Then Mrs. Lopez bends down, I figure to pick up the scale. When she stands up and I can see her face, I see fury.

What the fuck is with this lady? And who the hell is she to freaking *weigh* Kemina? A prickle of anger starts up under my arms—can't say just why but when I get pissed, I feel it first in my armpits—and it quickly spreads to my chest. Even with the constrictive sports bra I wear, I feel like my heart is gonna burst right out of my chest cavity.

If I'd thought the woman was pissed-off at the sound of the bed being moved before, well, it *ain't nothin'* compared to what I see right now. Freaking poison darts are shooting out of this lady's eyes like she's some kind of evil, highly evolved Pokémon. And she's not screaming, like before. Her fury is silent and septic; it emanates directly from her eyes and right into Kemina's. Shouted words are totally unnecessary—in fact, they'd be overkill. After about thirty seconds of this visual vitriol, Mrs. Lopez says one short sentence to Kemina, who nods in response.

My instinct is to get to Kemina and to run that angry bitch right out of the room. But I can't very easily do that now, can I? Inches of glass and a three-story drop separate us. And Kemina might tell me to take a hike cuz this woman is clearly her mother.

Her mother.

I've grown to detest the word. All kinds of negative personal experience with mothers will do that to somebody.

When Mrs. Lopez leaves, I sneak back into my bedroom. In the dark, I sit at my desk and then turn my chair toward the window to see what Kemi will do next. With that hollow expression I've come to recognize, Kemina strips down to her sports bra and booty shorts, dropping the clothes she'd worn to the café on her bedroom floor. She steps onto what turns out to be a mini-trampoline and she jumps. She then proceeds to jog and jump for the next half hour, throwing her arms into the frenzied movements, and soon her hips. Kemina is relentless, and I'd say for a minimum of thirty minutes she does not slow her pace.

I watch her drink from a bottle of water that is sitting on her bureau. She's thirsty and she sucks down more than half the bottle in one long sip. I know how that feels; sometimes I play b-ball so hard I forget I'm a senior at an all-girls high school in Manhattan playing streetball with my homies, and in my head I'm a power forward in the WNBA. But this girl is jumping on a trampoline, alone in her bedroom, a pained expression on her face. Kemi's not living through the awesome agony and the necessary joy and the life-giving force of physical activity—she's merely burning calories. She lifts a towel and with it dabs her face and neck and chest. And then she gets back on the trampoline. An hour later, when I hit the hay, she's still running on that thing.

9

I don't see Kemina for a few days. Her bedroom lights are always off, the curtains are closed, and I can tell that she hasn't been in there. But I've been busy with school, going to Bart and Joey's games, tons of AP US History homework, and shopping for our lunch date with the precious and perfect Princess Pam.

So Sunday comes, and about halfway through the morning, the boys and me get busy cooking. Jory and Jake are so freaking into this.

"For the salad, we've got tomatoes, cucumbers, onions, and, of course, lettuce," I tell them.

"Can we use the sharp knives?" Jazzed-bro looks a little bit too excited. "One of those knives could slice a piece of paper in half!"

"I think we can use our regular table knives." I see the supreme disappointment on his face, so I add, "except for on the tomatoes. They get all squishy if the knife is too dull. So we can slice the tomatoes together."

"Should we wash all of this stuff first? Don't want Pam to eat a bug, huh?" The look on Jory's face suggests that he might actually enjoy observing Pamela ingest a wriggling insect, but I don't call him on it mostly cuz I'd enjoy it, too.

"Everything is clean. Just put them on the chopping board and get busy."

I don't have to ask them twice.

It could be no clearer that the boys made the salad had they carved their names into the chunks—no, not slices—of cucumber. The lettuce is shredded into microscopic, uneven, and unrecognizable-as-salad slivers, the onions are diced so small they are mushy, the cucumber chunks are each more than a mouthful, however, the tomatoes slices look pretty good. But yeah, it's clearly a Jory-and-Jake's-kitchen-experiment kind of salad.

"We even made the dressing, Pam." Jake is barely able to contain his glee.

But when I glance at Pam, I get a sinking feeling in my stomach. She's staring at the salad as if it's a bowl of maggots to be consumed in a Survivor Challenge.

"We mixed up ketchup and mayonnaise. Justine's recipe."

This is when Pam wrinkles her puny nose. For the *first* time this meal.

"Oh, lovely," she chokes out. "But I'm afraid I'm just not in a salad kind of mood today."

My dad looks right at me when Pamela offers her polite refusal. He knows me well enough to figure that he might have to hold me back from taking a swing at his date due to her overly refined taste in chopped vegetables.

"Pamela, the salad looks delicious and the boys worked very hard on it." Yeah, Dad makes an effort to influence her to try the salad, but his voice is weak and what I'd classify as wimpy. I experience an urge to slug him, as well.

"I *said* I am *not* in the *mood*." Picky, plucky Pam. I bet my father's heard *that* line a time or two in regard to something else entirely….

I resist the urge to say, "Just eat the freaking salad, lady." Instead, despite my prickling armpits, I serve Dad and myself, and then the boys, giant helpings, and say, "Well, that means more salad for us, right guys?"

The twins are not happy about this turn of events cuz they had wanted to impress Pamela Perkins with their culinary genius. It looks to me as if someone popped Jake and the air is slowly leaking out of him. And Jory, well, Jory is a different story, altogether. The hostility that was gone for the past few days is back. And then some. I resist an urge to remove Jory's knife from the table, and instead just hope like hell he won't pitch it at our dinner guest.

"OMG!" I can hardly believe I just said that. I am *not* an OMG-girl at all. "I have never tasted salad so amazing. Have you, Dad?"

Dad is shoveling in the salad like he's a rabbit on steroids. "Absolutely not. May I *please* have seconds? I mean, I don't even have words to describe this salad!" He sounds as if he is sexually aroused by chopped veggies, which is G.R.O.S.S. in my humble opinion.

But at our enthusiasm, the boys perk up slightly.

The now-petulant Pam is staring into her empty salad bowl. "Please pass the bread," she pouts.

Nobody reaches for the cheesy garlic bread for like thirty seconds. Then Dad finally breaks down and grabs the breadbasket. "Here you go, Pammy."

10

Just got back from a shoot in Florida. A new line of swimsuits. It's all done and I'm STARVING!! Meet me at Naldo's Café?

Kemina keeps food hidden in her third from the bottom dresser drawer. I know this cuz she just pulled it open, pushed over a bunch of sweaters or something, and voila—she's opening one of those packages of peanut butter and crackers and then stuffing them into her mouth two at a time. Kemi comes to the window, holds the sign up in one hand, stuffs her face with the other, and kind of glances nervously at her bedroom door every couple of seconds. I know she's worried that her mom will barge in with a freaking tape measure and a red marker in her hands, all set to pinch an inch of her butt or belly fat and then mark and measure it like she's a plastic surgeon. And catch her eating—

holy crap—*Ritz crackers*!! Which would be a sin beyond comprehension.

I will admit that the emaciated-model look that Kemi is rockin' brings to my mind something disturbing. And whenever this image creeps into my brain I try like hell to shove it out, but sometimes you just can't control the musing of your mind.

Mom. Yup. There it is.

I look at Kemi's bony shoulders and sunken-in cheeks and hands that look oversized on frail wrists and I think of my alcoholic stoner of a mother. All that's missing is a reddish nose, a bloated belly, and some facial scabs, and Kemi would have successfully achieved the appearance of a malnourished druggy boozer. But there's a difference. When I think of Kemi I don't experience a complicated and painful blend of emotions—pity and disgust and anger and rejection and loss all wrapped into one pathetic package. When I think of Kemi's little battle with forced starvation, it's more like—*this poor girl needs a Panini with a side of sweet potato fries and a strawberry frappe, heavy on the ice cream.*

And I am the perfect person to provide her with these things.

Half an hour?

I scribble and hold up my sketchpad.

She actually winks and grins. This creature is so excited by the prospect of filling her empty belly that she is a winking, grinning fool.

And I'll be all in black, she writes. No surprise there. *Look for a Yankees cap.*

I cringe very slightly as I'm *not* a Yankees fan, but this is Kemina's disguise, not mine, and I'm willing to accept anything that works for her.

I flash my final sign.

Can't freaking wait.

I receive another wink. I wink back but she's already turned away.

Kemina Lopez can certainly put down deep-dish pizza with the best of them. She really ought to enter some kind of citywide pizza-eating contest. For a split second I imagine Kemina, all decorated in her naughty Green Vixen lingerie, sitting at a long table along with four burly dudes on either side of her, ready to sink her teeth into the first of many pizza pies. Her eyes are wild and hungry, just like they were back in her bedroom a little while ago, prior to the peanut-butter-cracker-crime she committed against her mother.

Kemina's moan of pleasure at the first bite of her fourth slice brings me back to Naldo's Café.

"So I take it you like pizza?"

Kemina roughly wipes her mouth with her wrist. It is such a raw and feral gesture, not controlled and calculated like I'm used to from her, that it sends an instant jolt of sexual awareness into my mind, and my body too, if I'm gonna be honest. "You could say that." Another bite. Another soft moan. *Yeah.*

"I think we chose our seats right today." Carrying our pizza and smoothies on a big tray, I had followed her upstairs to the loft—to the far back corner, but on the opposite side from the restrooms. She knows how to do this—how to hide in plain sight. "How long have you had to put up with all of the cameras and the questions?"

"Only since October when I signed the contract with Nightingale to be the Green Vixen. That was when I turned eighteen."

"And before that?"

"I modeled for Always Young Outfitters. Back then mainly only teenagers recognized me. But being a Vixen, it is like I'm on the map, all of a sudden."

"And who you date matters?"

Kemina nods and dives back into her pizza. She never seems to want to talk about personal stuff.

"What was up with all of the exercising last week? You know, on the trampoline."

She sighs and drops the crust of her pizza onto the white paper plate. "Calorie burning. I had gained almost two pounds and that isn't cool before a bikini photo shoot." Kemi sighs again, and then she shrugs in defeat. "The pizza I just ate spells like three hours on the treadmill at the gym."

"That's warped." I didn't really think about saying that. Sometimes things just pop out of my mouth.

"Well, *I* support us—Mama and me. And she always says stuff like, 'Your muffin top could cost us our home.'"

"That's a lot of pressure."

Again the nod, but her eyes haven't gone hollow yet. "I've been dealing with it for years, but it's worse since I turned eighteen. I can show the world more skin now, which translates into I can have less fat on my body."

"Drink your smoothie," I say, pushing it toward her. "You've gotta wash that pizza down with something. Plus, the bikini shoot is over. "

"There's always another one right around the corner." But she lifts the cup to her lips, and while she's drinking the smoothie, I kind of drink in the sight of her. She looks younger and cuter than usual today in that baseball cap. I choose to ignore the Yankees logo. When she's finished I suggest we go for a walk.

We leave the café and, without a plan, start walking north on Broadway.

"You're graduating this spring, too, so what are you going to do next year?" She asks.

"Already applied and been accepted to Marymount Manhattan, cuz they have rolling admissions. I'm gonna major in business—or that's the plan."

Kemina gets that hungry look in her eyes again. "I'd love to go to City College of New York. There are two programs there that I'm interested in—Latino Studies and Women's Studies—but Mama wants me to put college on hold for a while."

"Why?" I ask.

"She says I'm only gonna be young and beautiful for a short window of time and we need to cash in on it."

Kemina has a crappy mother in an entirely different way than I do. "I think you should still apply."

"I took the SATs. Was late to a shoot because of them." She chuckles after she says it, but I can tell it wasn't a funny situation at all. "Mama nearly lost her marbles."

"Just apply to college, Kemi. What is it? Like sixty dollars, an application, a recommendation or two, your transcript, SATs, and an essay—it can't hurt."

Kemi's hungry eyes turn into wistful ones. "It's really close to the application deadline, Justine. Maybe even past it."

I send her a look that suggests I'm not buying her BS, and I say, "I think City College takes students until all of the spots are filled up."

Kemina nods and replies in a slightly aloof tone, "Well, maybe I will apply."

Then she pulls me close to her side, hooks her arm into mine, and speeds up the pace of our walking. Suddenly I feel like I'm on a real date.

11

The idea of going on a real date with Kemina gets stuck in my head. All I can think of is taking her somewhere cool, both of us stylin' in our nicest clothes, and getting to know each other better while we're doing something fun and interesting. She probably wouldn't be totally sure if we were on a date or just two friends hanging out, but it would be a step in the right direction. I'd be showing her a good time, and it would be in a much more formal way than meeting at Naldo's or holding up signs in a window. Which is much more like a real date.

I get this awesome idea. Thursday is a teacher's workshop, and UWSAA students have the day off school. So before I go to bed on Wednesday night, I leave my sketchpad on the windowsill, a note with specific instructions printed neatly on it. She'll see it whenever she gets home.

If you can get away tomorrow, meet me @ 11AM at the Museum of Modern Art on West 53rd Street. You can't miss it— it's a shiny glass building with MoMA written in huge letters down the side. Let's dress up! And arrive hungry, cuz we'll get lunch.

I'm pretty convinced that if Kemina's available she'll be there tomorrow. I fall asleep with my fingers crossed, hoping so hard she'll show up.

I can't miss her—nobody with eyes could. Despite the long black overcoat and dark scarf draped over her loose hair, I can tell she's dressed up, and I can't help but blush because I know she's all dressed up for *me.* She wears these funky strappy, kinda badass black heels, and I can see a lacy dark green dress beneath, as her coat has blown open. And I really like every inch of what I see. I've gone with the Ellen DeGeneres-goes-formal-look, which includes my best white button-down, a maroon velvet suit jacket with narrow, black pants, and, of course, I rock a multicolored bow tie for the formal, we're-on-a-date, effect.

So maybe I wanna impress the bejesus outta the girl.

"You look perfect," I say as soon as she's within hearing distance, and Kemi tilts her head as if to think about what I just said, and finally she smiles. I wish the smile was serene, but there's a tension it in I can't miss. She looks all around her as if expecting to have been followed, and I think I know the source of her anxiety. So, I grab her hand, and pull her toward the entrance before any overly nosy people with big cameras show up on the sidewalk. "Let's go inside."

No one follows us.

Interestingly, we invest the bulk of our time in the airy halls of MoMA checking out images of women. We spend a long while with our eyes glued to Paul Gauguin's Polynesian goddess in *The Seed of the Areoi,* and we decide she is the artist's idea of perfect beauty. Gauguin uses bright colors and exaggerated body proportions that surprisingly make his model look something less than delicate. But she's still very beautiful. And after that, for almost an hour, we check out Henri de Toulouse-Lautrec's art, that seems to focus on his ideal—red-haired women. It's easy to tell that what he finds fascinating is the lack of glamour in the seemingly glitzy lives of ladies working in dancehalls and brothels. The expression in Kemina's eyes tells me that she can relate to the women Toulouse-Lautrec shows in his art.

Pablo Picasso's art definitely captures the largest share of Kemina's attention, though. In silence, we study the solid and even chunky bodies of the women in *Two Nudes* for what seems like the longest time.

Finally, Kemina asks me, "Do you think Picasso finds these women beautiful?"

It takes me a few minutes to come up with my answer. "I think he finds them notable and true... and worthy to be subjects of his art." I consider what she's asking me a bit more and then add, "And really womanly."

Kemina nods slowly and her wrinkled forehead tells me she's thinking very seriously about what she's seeing here today. I'm pretty sure I could guess what's weighing on her mind—that beautiful women come in all sizes and shapes—but I don't. If she wants to discuss it, she'll bring it up.

There's a bunch of people standing around the Picasso piece called *Girl Before a Mirror,* so we have to wait for a while until we can get close enough to fully take it in. In this one, Picasso's model's body parts are all separated and broken apart, but you can somehow tell that he thinks the girl he has depicted is beautiful and sexy and very alive. But what the girl sees in the mirror when she gazes at herself is somehow sad and distorted, not at all in line with what the world sees when they look at her.

"Why does she see herself that way?" Kemina asks, but I don't think she expects an answer so I keep my mouth shut. And my gaze is again drawn to Kemi's face—a mask of contemplation. It's as if she's trying to figure out the answer to a riddle.

On the second floor, MoMA has a small restaurant called Café 2. I buy each of us sandwiches and then get mocha lattes from the espresso bar, and we choose our usual in-the-back-corner seating. When we sit down and gaze at each other over the table, Kemina appears like she is in deep thought. And every once in a while, she looks all around her. I find myself wondering why.

I pass Kemina her plate from off the tray and say to her softly, "I don't think the paparazzi know we're here. So, no worries, 'kay?"

Kemina shakes her head. In the dark green dress, her eyes are as vivid as the grass in Central Park on a bright summer day, and they're very wide when she replies, "I'm not looking for photographers."

I glance around us and suddenly I know what she's looking at.

Mothers and daughters. They seem to be everywhere.

I see little girls—maybe homeschooled kids—and their attentive mommies, in scattered groups, seemingly all sharing in some kind of a big joke, judging by their frequent laughter. There are young women in their late teens and early twenties sitting at tables across from their mothers, pleased to be engaged in animated adult discussions of art. And there are older women and their elderly moms, heads leaning in toward each other over their cups of tea, all consumed with cozy conversation.

Neither of us have this type of bond with our own mothers. I don't think Kemina *ever* did, though I may have had a little slice of this intimacy with Mom when I was a kid. The jury is out as to whether either of us will have this closeness with our mothers in the future.

"You're looking at the mothers and daughters?"

Kemi doesn't even nod. We both know the answer to my question.

"It just isn't like this," she looks around the room, "with Mama and me."

"I know." I can only agree.

"I wish it were. I've tried since I was a young girl to smooth things out with her. To be the person she wants me to be."

Kemina stops talking and looks around the café one more time. "I really did try."

"That's pretty obvious to me, Kemi."

"Some people, even some mothers, just can't be pleased… it seems." She shrugs and lifts her sandwich to her lips and holds it there. "Speaking of Mama, she'd chop my hands off if she knew I was putting *this* in my mouth."

I'm not sure whether it's appropriate to laugh, mainly cuz I suspect Kemina isn't joking, so I just agree with her. "Yeah." And I think of my own mother. No matter how hard I try to block her out, I just can't. She's always right there on the edges of my awareness, surrounded by layers of pain. The thing is, I know it isn't so much that Mom would *purposely* hold back the kind of closeness I see around me in order to hurt or manipulate me. She just *can't* give it to me. It's like Mom is missing some behavioral chip in her personality that allows her to prioritize her kids over her booze, and whatever else she uses. So no matter what Mom's reasons for neglecting me, I think I probably feel as robbed of this whole motherly-love thing as Kemi does.

"Well, I'll chop your hands of if you put that sandwich down, Kemi, so eat!" And I wouldn't say she dives right in, but she does take a delicate bite. Her eyes close a bit when she tastes the spicy flavor, and I know she likes it.

For a few minutes we linger over our sandwiches, and our conversation is suspended. During this time, I somehow muster up my courage, and I reach out with my boat-shoed foot to touch her sexy sandaled one. When my foot meets Kemi's, I can tell she's slipped hers out of the sandal, so I toe off my boat shoe. And our bare toes come together. Kemina's foot is cool and silky and *very* receptive. I shiver from the intimate contact. She does too.

Kemi leans over the table toward me and says in a breathy tone, "I've been thinking a lot about perfection, when it comes to visual beauty, since coming to this museum today."

"So have I," I admit. "But tell me what you think first."

She takes a sip of her mocha latte and dabs her lips with her napkin. "When I think about the way these artists view the ideal woman, I realize that there's no single standard for beauty. Their ideas of *perfect* are all over the map."

I wait for more.

"Like take Picasso, for example…. You can tell that he sees incredible beauty in the women he paints. And they're not tall and skinny as a rail like what seems to be the standard of perfection in today's world. In fact, they're heavy and clunky and… and a very solid sort of lovely."

I fully agree with her conclusion, but I have something to add. "Some of his paintings don't even resemble a real woman at all. He just sees parts and pieces of a lady's whole, and finds beauty there."

"It makes me wonder what I've been dedicating my entire life to. Whose idea of perfect am I trying to live up to?"

"Maybe the whole 'perfect' thing is really subjective," I hadn't anticipated that our date to the Museum of Modern Art would turn out to be quite this significant to Kemina. But I'm glad for both of us, to say the least. Together, we're discovering new and important truths.

She reaches across the table and takes my hand almost roughly, not even looking around to see who's watching us. This impulsive gesture means an incredible amount to me. "When you first saw me today you said I looked perfect, and I was actually insulted because I so badly don't want you to be as shallow as the rest of the world."

"You mean, you don't want me to judge you on just your appearance?"

"Yeah. And, you know, you saying I'm perfect because of what you see just hit me as …."

I put her worries to rest as best I can. "It's just that you're perfect to me, Kemina, cuz beauty truly is in the eye of the beholder, don't you think?"

"It is, Justine." We're on the very same page, which is cool.

I think of Toulouse-Lautrec and his red-haired women and Gauguin and his Polynesian goddess. And then I think of Kemina, who is almost everybody's idea of perfect, but the things I like best about her are the parts of her that aren't really perfect at all. Like the crookedness of her smile that she only shows on those rare occasions when she allows herself to really let go and grin, and her smart mouth that lets me know she can be honest with me, sometimes brutally so, and even the shadows in her eyes that make me hope *only I* can push them away.

"This has been an amazing day," she tells me. "It lets me know I can look at everything differently."

I seriously hope she's started looking at me as her girlfriend and not just her friend who happens to be a girl. Somehow, though, I think she's referring to things more profound than how she views her relationship with Justine Laraby.

"I'm glad you had fun. I did too," I reply.

"Thank you for taking me here." Kemina's beautiful emerald gaze is fixed on my face. "Maybe we can go to another art museum someday."

I'm nodding before I even realize it. And that's when she pulls her hand from mine, and reaches up to touch my cheek. For a second, as her fingers linger on the side of my face, her eyes drop toward the table. But in almost no time at all, they again lift, and she's looking at me. Like I really matter to her.

This is all I ever hoped for when I planned this date. *More than, really....*

We stay like this for a long moment, and then she takes her hand back from my face, stands up, and says, "Let's go look at The Sculpture Garden."

I take to my feet and grab our tray. "I've been to The Sculpture Garden before. I think you're gonna love this Maillol sculpture called *The River*. It's super huge—of a *very curvy* woman—and it looks like she's moving. She's all twisted and turning and… well, come on." Kemina follows me from the café.

12

I cannot freaking believe I'm doing this.

So after the fiasco that was Sunday dinner, Dad told me he "gently suggested" to Pamela that she "put herself out there" a bit more with his kids. So the suddenly playful Pamela starts her attempt to "put herself out there" with *me*—the little doll.

Anyway, here I am at *Pampered and Polished Nail Salon* in Soho, my feet soaking in a bucket of warm sudsy water and the fingers of my right hand fanned out under this probably-cancer-causing-supersonic-nail-drying contraption. But I have struggled through my fight-or-flight-response and I'm proud to say that I'm still here in the beauty trenches. With newly French tipped fingernails and, I'm thinking, maybe I'll get some shade of blue on my toenails. I'm not going to commit to it yet, but there's one color called "Lady Sings the Blues" that isn't half-bad.

What I do for love…well, for Dad's lover.

I don't cry like I did during my last manicure experience at Lani's first grade girly birthday party that I bailed out of, and neither do I call Dad and plead with him to come pick me up and return me to the safety of my OKC Thunder-themed bedroom. Instead, I grit my teeth, spread out my fingers, and let Filippe, the manicurist, have his way with me.

Joey, Bart, and the other guys are gonna laugh their asses off later at the YMCA when I attempt to palm the basketball with French tipped nails.

This one's for you, Dad. I hope you and the twins appreciate my sacrifice.

"So, Justine, tell me… have you set your sites on a nice young fellow? You are a very pretty girl. We just need to do something with your hair." She turns and gawks at me—and yes, she wrinkles that tiny freckled nose—right from her foot-soaking throne beside mine. "With your hair as it is now, you resemble that troublemaking boy pop vocalist, um, what's his name?"

Filippe chimes in with, "Justin Bieber."

I fight with every ounce of my inner strength not to roll my eyes. And I still fail.

"Yes, that's the one." She reaches over and pulls the hair up off one side of my face and I feel so exposed. "Maybe a pretty up-do would make a boy lose his eyes for you… You have lovely high cheek bones, doll—you *really* shouldn't hide them."

"'Tis a crime to hide fine bone structure such as this." Filippe is *not* being helpful here.

But I'm here on business, I remind myself, *just as newly-playful, freshly-polished Pam is.* This is not a social event, contrary to Filippe's naïve understanding of this apparent mother-daughter salon trip. *I* am on a mission to save my brothers from heartache; *she* is on a mission to trap a man. "So Pam, next time the boys make you food… um, my suggestion is that you find a way to choke it down."

Is that too blunt?

Pam raises her "Beets Me Red" painted fingernails to her now O-shaped lips, as if surprised by my words, but she doesn't fool me. "I simply wasn't experiencing a craving for salad on Sunday, doll. It's not a crime."

I ignore her excuse and continue my instructions. "My father *loves* those boys. Bottom line, Pammy—you ain't gonna get anywhere with the man unless you take Jake and Jory along for the ride. You made a strategic error last Sunday with your fake lachanophobia, but I think you already know that."

She's not yet ready to admit her guilt. "Lachanophobia?" To throw me off, Perplexed Pam makes an appearance. She wrinkles her tiny nose in confusion. "What on earth is that?"

"Fear of vegetables." I don't remember where I picked up this random piece of information, not that it matters. "Salad avoidance, and I think you know what I'm talking about." I knit my eyebrows together in an attempt to look fierce. I will say that this is the first time I've ever wished sincerely that I had a unibrow, cuz everybody knows that unibrows are freaking intimidating. "You may even find that you like the two little guys. They aren't nearly as despicable as you think."

Filippe hesitates in the application of a fine white tip to the nail of my left hand's index finger in order to check out Pam's reaction to my flippancy. I can't resist. I reach forward and close his dangling jaw with my Un-French tipped pointer.

"Well, I...." She needs a second to gather her thoughts.

I strike again quickly, refusing to allow her the chance to build a defense. "On Friday night, the boys and Dad are going to invite you to go ice skating and then over to our place for hot cocoa and cookies. Cookies that the boys and I will be making, with our very own *filthy* fingers on Thursday night." Filippe looks scandalized. *Buckle up, Filippe, cuz this is where it's gonna get bumpy.* "You will be there. You will eat cookies—and plenty of them. You will gush on and on about the amazingness of the cookies. You will beg to take a Ziploc baggy of them home so you can eat half a dozen more before you go to bed."

Passive Pam nods.

Filippe nods.

I nod.

And so it is settled.

13

Her cheeks aren't so hollow lately, and neither is the expression in her eyes. This probably makes me feel just a little bit too good, seeing as we're mere acquaintances and not girlfriends.

Window pen pals speaking in sign language is what we are.

Right now Kemi is sneaky-eating again. That's how I think of it, at least. She's sitting cross-legged on the middle of her bed facing the window, her bakery bag of some kind of chocolate cookies hidden underneath her pillow, and she's filling her face with a certain urgency, occasionally looking back at her bedroom door with these guilty basset hound eyes. So, yeah, I'm happy she's eating, but I'm also pissed that she has to do it on the down-low. Like she's some kind of pastry-eating criminal.

What I'm happiest about, in a kind of selfish way, is that Kemi no longer has the gaunt, I'm-addicted-to-illegal-substances look that my mother had when I saw her last summer. That most recent meeting with Mom pretty much messed me up for the entire month of July, and the twins had a really hard time with it, too. Looking into Mom's eyes, that incidentally seemed way too big for her gray-skinned face, and staring at her emaciated body, was like getting visual proof that my mother's priorities were *so* not her kids. And maybe she *was* sorry, and maybe she *couldn't* help it, and maybe she *would* try to change—which were all the claims she'd made to me and the boys that muggy summer day— but that doesn't change the fact that she's gone, has been gone for five years, and was mentally gone, even back when she was physically living with us.

And for some unknown reason, seeing a person in that condition—particularly someone I care about despite the bullshit—brings on the heavy guilt. As if grade school Justine could have somehow stopped her mom from taking that first drink that led to the second and then the third, which ultimately drove her to doing all the drugs and leaving home... and finally living only for her next chance to get high.

So seeing Kemina as she is now, pink-cheeked instead of sallow, and looking stronger than she does fragile, with an expression of *having* instead of *wanting*, wipes the thoughts of my mother away. And my mind is cleansed of that particular pain until the next reminder seeps into my brain.

So I'm just lounging on my bed, holding a book but making no effort to hide the fact that I'm studying her, when Kemina gets a phone call. She lifts her phone to her ear, and upon hearing the voice, turns away from me slightly. When she turns back, she's smiling. Nah—she's grinning. And it's a goofy sort of grin—the crooked one. I like it.

After the call, Kemi places the phone on her bed and grabs her notebook. When she holds it up, I can't believe what I'm reading.

Come over to my apartment.

I sit up and cross my legs, just like her. But I don't respond cuz I'm floored.

She nods at me, and points at the sign again.

I somehow locate my brain and grab my sketchpad off the night table.

What's your apartment number?

2-B

We're scribbling words as fast as we can.

What about your mother?

Mama's out all night. ☺ *Just buzz and I'll let you in.*

My breathing—well, all I can say is that it isn't in…out…in….out… anymore. It's all staggered and I feel like I have to think about inhaling and exhaling to make it happen. Cuz I'm going to be alone with Kemina.

Give me five minutes.

And just like that, I'm up and off to the bathroom, where I brush my teeth, throw some water on my face, and comb my hair. I glance in the mirror, see a reasonably tidy facsimile of Justin Bieber staring back at me. I spray a bit of Axe on my T-shirt, and I'm off.

Kemina's room smells floral, like Nightingale's Vixen Blume perfume, I assume, not that this discovery is in any way surprising. When I ask about the scent, she tells me she gets free samples of the Blume fragrance on Vixen photo shoots and is encouraged by the company to wear it. Kemi smells really good, too. She smells soft and sweet—like outdoors in the spring—so I think she's wearing some kind of Nightingale perfume, as well. I can tell that she likes flowers in general, as there are flowers everywhere in her room. Her bedspread—lilacs. Her throw pillows—daisies. The wall art—wild flowers. Her scatter rugs—

roses. It's distracting and maybe even overwhelming to be surrounded so entirely by this visual flower garden. It makes me feel small and a little bit lost, and it suddenly hits me that may be Kemina's purpose in setting her room up this way.

She pulls the light peach curtains closed so we have privacy, although there's no one in *my* bedroom peering in at us cuz I'm here with her. And I notice that there is no lock on her bedroom door. She's apparently not entitled to privacy at home. I like "Mama Lopez" less and less by the minute.

"Wanna sit on my bed, Justine? We can mess around on my laptop."

Mess around.... If I was an "OMG" kind of girl, "we can mess around" would be on instant replay in my head right now, and I'd probably be squealing. "Yeah, sure."

I plunk my ass down on a cheerful daisy pillow and Kemina sort of floats over beside me. Then I swallow so loud we both can hear the sound. I'm just not too sure what to expect. I can't say *been there, done that* in regard to sitting with a girl on her bed in her sweet-smelling, flowery bedroom... alone.

"So what are we gonna watch...like...on your laptop?" I cannot believe I'm actually distracting Kemi from the fact that we're within easy kissing distance from each other.

"How about we check out cute baby animals?" She lifts her chin up and I look into her deep green eyes that are, incidentally, so much more stunning when she's this close to me. And they're so innocent—close up, I can tell that her eyes don't hold as many sensual secrets as I'd thought when I looked at her on the poster in the subway. Right now I don't see hollow and I don't see seductive and I don't really even see playful. Right now I see a kind of youthfulness I didn't know she was capable of.

"That's exactly what I was hoping you'd say."

And that's what we do. With tons of laughter—I'm not going to admit to all of the giggling—we look at kittens and puppies and piglets and ducklings, and soon we get a bit more adventurous and we check out baby hedgehogs and owls—*jeez, they're cute*—and then skunks and squirrels. By the time we get to the baby giraffes and elephants, Kemina is leaning heavily on my left arm and we aren't laughing anymore, and when we move on to baby sea creatures, my arm is around her and you could hear a pin drop in the room.

But it's not until the screen fills with the image of this baby seal, all white and fluffy with dark vulnerable eyes that we both gasp a little bit and then turn to look at each other. I can feel her breath on my lips and my nose is nearly touching hers, and, well, I don't know about Kemina, but I'm all kinds of spellbound by this moment. She reaches up and touches my jaw, just below my ear, with this soft brush of her fingertips, and I have no choice but to lean down and kiss her. Not that I was looking too hard for another option. Cuz I wasn't.

I kind of thought that my first kiss would be like an electric shock or the sharp poke of cupid's dart or fireworks exploding in a dark night sky, but it's not like any of those things. The way it feels when my lips touch Kemina's is soft and gentle and tender. It's a yielding of her mouth to mine, and then mine to hers. It's an intimate moment that's breathy and warm and sweet and just ours.

"Ummmm...." She lets out this sound that makes me think of how it feels to sink into a hot bath after a long afternoon of ice skating in frigid temperatures. "That was my first *real* kiss."

"*Real* kiss?" I ask. Our lips are only about an inch apart. I have a strong feeling that her second *real* kiss is only a moment away.

"I've done acting kinds of kisses, you know, with boys on sets... for shoots. But not ones with the girl I've been waiting for forever. Not a kiss," she touches her lips to mine and I can feel her sureness, "like this," one more time, a bit more firmly, she presses her mouth to mine, "with you."

Kemina then pulls me down so we're lying beside each other on the narrow bed. She flips onto her side so her butt is up against my hips and she pushes her back against my chest. The only right thing to do is to wrap my arms around her. Her shoulders feel narrower than they look, and my hands come to rest on her belly.

Spooning.

I am spooning the most beautiful, softest, sweetest girl in the world, who places her hands on top of mine and squeezes to let me know she's feeling it too. "Wish you could stay... or that I could go with you." She says it in a dreamy tone, and somehow I know that her eyes are closed.

And I wonder about the second part of what she said until from downstairs we hear a banging sound that I recognize as the slamming of a door. Kemina's entire body stiffens in my arms. "Is that your mom?"

Before answering, she hops up from the bed and straightens her clothes. I do the same. "Yeah, that's Mama. I have no idea why she's back so soon—we were just studying, okay?"

"Right." I'm not exactly planning to tell Mrs. Lopez that I was spooning her daughter and thoroughly enjoying it.

"Come on." I follow her down the stairs, and since the apartment is set up identically to ours, when we stop walking I know we're right outside of their kitchen. Kemina turns to me, lifts my hand to her lips and kisses my fingertips. I wonder if she notices my French tipped nails, and I'm sure I blush because of that, but I don't pull my hand away because I'm too psyched about what she's doing. Then she lets go of my hand and it's time to meet her mother.

The Kemina who walks into the kitchen is a totally different one than I kissed on the bed in the sweet-smelling upstairs bedroom. The little light of warmth that had snapped on behind her eyes is now in the off position, and she sort of drags her feet as she approaches her mother. When Kemi slouches her shoulders, I can tell she has closed herself off to the world. This transition of her entire person would have been fascinating to witness, had it not been so sad.

Once we're beside her in the kitchen, Mrs. Lopez gapes at Kemi, and gestures toward me with her elbow. "Who's that?"

"This is Justine Laraby, Mama. She lives next door."

"What's she doing here?" Her voice is as hollow as Kemi's eyes.

"We were studying."

Kemina's mother smiles, but it's a wicked one, and I can tell that she doesn't believe her daughter. "Like hell, you were."

We all stand there staring at each other. I find my voice, but it's a bit more challenging to find my positive attitude. "It's nice to meet you. Mrs. Lopez." I say it without expression.

Mrs. Lopez looks me up and down, and there's a shit ton of ice in her stare. Then she turns toward Kemi, and asks, "Did you exercise?"

"I… I'm going to the gym tomorrow."

"That's *not* what I asked you." When Kemina doesn't say anything else, Mrs. Lopez nods toward the stairs. "Well, what are you waiting for, Kemina? Go back upstairs and get busy on your trampoline. You have a shoot coming up, or were you 'studying' so hard you forgot?" She makes those air quotes with her fingers. I frigging detest air quotes, more now than ever.

"It's a shoot for jeans, not swimsuits or—"

"Say good-bye to your…your *friend*." I can't help but stare from Mrs. Lopez to her daughter, sizing them up, trying to figure out how Kemina got her sweetness from this hard-edged woman.

I step in at this point. "I've got homework, anyway, so I… I know where the door is. I can let myself out."

Neither of them acknowledges that I said anything. They're fully occupied by some kind of demented mother-daughter staring contest. Kemina is the one to look away first. But without meeting my eyes, she says, "No, let me walk you to the door, Justine."

"No, really, it's okay. I can find my way out." I barely finish speaking and Kemina is on her way back to the stairs.

14

I come home from Bart's basketball game about halfway through the cookie-devouring part of Pamela, Dad, and the boys' Friday night get-together. Pragmatic Pamela is doing me proud. She's clearly taken my sensible advice, and is chowing down on peanut-butter-chocolate-drop cookies like she's never before seen food. Dad is gazing at her fondly, and I can literally see that he is falling a little bit more in love with her with each cookie she puts down, which makes me throw up a little in my mouth, but I suppose it's all good. And as they watch Pam shoveling their homemade cookies into her pie hole by the handful—barely taking time to chew one mouthful before shoving in another—Jake and Jory's dark eyes light up just the way they do when they come downstairs on Christmas morning and see their presents under the tree.

So, all in all, it's a charming homey scene.

I sigh.

"Jussy, come on and have some cookies and cocoa with us," Jake urges, adding in a low voice, "cuz if ya don't grab some cookies now, I'm thinking Pam's gonna polish 'em off and there won't be none left."

I walk over to the kitchen table where parched Pam is now sucking down hot cocoa with gusto, bringing to mind a weary traveler who has crossed the Sahara Desert without the benefit of a canteen. I ruffle up Jake's hair and then Jory's, and I say, "Just ate pizza with the guys. Couldn't fit a cookie in my belly if my life depended on it."

Pam burps quietly, excuses herself, and then our eyes meet. Hers are strangely wide.

"How was skating, guys?" I ask them, but look straight at her.

"We had a blast!" Jake blurts.

"Pam can twirl around!" Even Jory is pumped. "*Ten* times in a row!"

My father reaches over and wipes Pamela's adorable little hot cocoa mustache from her upper lip. He beams at her, and utters wistfully, "If we keep having family times like this, Pammy might be a keeper."

Way to put all your cards on the table, Dad.

Pamela blushes and then grins in this got-what-I-wanted way.

And I want to scream, "What's the hurry, Dad? Slow the heck down!" But I suppose he's been alone for a long time and it hasn't been much fun for him. And maybe he likes her, too.

There is that.

"Well, there's no need to save any cookies for me. So, have a field day polishing off the PB choc-drops, Pam." I wink at Pam, and despite her slightly nauseated expression, she winks back. I think she's catching on to this bonding-with-the-boys thing.

Up in my room, it's more of the same when I glance across the alley. A dark room—nobody's home. I can't help but wonder where Kemi's been all week. And then I wonder when or if we'll ever be alone again. So maybe I have nothing to compare that kiss to seeing as it was my first one, but I know it was better than what I ever expected or hoped a kiss would be. I also know that I want another one so badly I can actually taste it. And one more thing I realize is that this train of thought is getting me nowhere, and I'd better crack open the books because my homework awaits.

After spending about forty-five minutes on calculus problems, a light in the bedroom across the alley draws my attention. Trying not to be too obvious, I move from my desk to the bed, carrying my AP US History textbook and a highlighter as if I'm going to read, rather than what I'm really going to do— spy.

Kemi and her mom *both* enter the room, which admittedly causes my heart to sink. Mrs. Lopez leads Kemina to the bed, grasping her by the forearm. With visible disgust, she tosses a fist full of what appears to be mail onto Kemi's floral bedspread, grabs Kemina's face in her hand to force her to look at the messy pile, and starts ranting. Kemina makes no attempt to say anything. She just stands there, her cheeks held in a vice grip, staring at the envelopes scattered all over her bed, as if she's in some sort of a mail-induced daze.

After several minutes of this forced staring, Mrs. Lopez lets go of Kemina's face, gathers up all of the envelopes on the bed, walks to the door, again glares, and delivers one more verbal punch to Kemi. As her daughter recovers from whatever her mother last said, she leaves without a backward glance. And Kemi stands like she's frozen to the floor, gawking at her bed as if the mail is still scattered there. And she's wearing a bright red finger and thumbprint on her cheeks—can't forget those details. At least a full five minutes pass before she takes a step forward and crumples onto the bed on her stomach.

I want so badly to fly across the alley so that I can ask her what's wrong and help her figure out how to make it right. But a big part of me knows that this situation is nowhere near that simple. So, instead, I grab my sketchbook and my royal blue marker and I write.

When Kemi finally lifts her head from the bed, her eyes are puffy, as she was clearly crying. She looks in my direction and I waste no time. I hop up off my bed and press my sign to the window.

Do you know how to get onto the roof?

She nods, and I see that hollow look in her eyes, which is exaggerated by all of the smeared mascara.

Go up on your building's roof and I'll go up on mine. We can talk.

She sits up on her bed and shrugs as if she isn't sure. So I write again.

Let me help you.

Again she shrugs as if helping her is a lost cause, but then she nods, so I drop the sketchpad and marker on the bed and I head for my building's back stairway. Kemina shows up on the roof in about ten minutes. It's pretty dark, but I can see that her face has been scrubbed clean of all the dripping makeup, and she looks younger than usual. Spring is approaching, and thankfully, it isn't bitterly cold up here, though it is a bit windy. She tucks her blowing hair underneath her long black coat. We both move to the railings at the edges of the roof so we can be as close as possible to each other.

I wait for a while to see if she'll speak first, but she doesn't say anything, or even look at me. So I break the ice, but I have to use a kinda loud voice to do it. "You were gone all week."

Kemina glances across the alley at me. "I had a shoot—it was out of town."

"I looked for you every night, but the lights were always off."

She doesn't comment on my observation.

"What was going on in your bedroom before? With your mom?"

Again, no response.

"You don't have to tell me."

"I know I don't." Her tone is curt.

This is like pulling freaking teeth. "I wanna try to help you figure it all out. But I can't if I've got no clue what's up."

She sighs and it's pretty loud cuz I can hear it across the alley on a blustery night. "Mama was angry. I was asked to leave the photo shoot yesterday."

"Jeez. Was it a shoot for Vixen lingerie?" I can't imagine Kemi getting booted out of anywhere.

Kemina shakes her head. "No. It was for jeans. Nash Denim."

I'm a Levi's girl through and through, but I've heard of Nash Denim. Real high end, as in, a couple hundred dollars a pair. "Why? Why did they ask you to leave?"

Kemi is quiet for so long I start to doubt she's ever gonna answer. Then she says, in a monotone voice, "The size two jeans were way too snug on me, and they didn't have size fours on location. The photographer told me I was looking like a plus-size model." She drops her head into her hands. "He told me not to come back to Nash until my ass wasn't the size of a house."

I get the underarm-prickling-angry feeling. "That's freaking absurd!"

"Well, it's exactly what happened." Kemina's voice is muffled by the wind. "And no work, no pay."

"That's why your mother was pissed?"

"Uh huh." She looks up again. "Those were our bills that she threw on my bed. If I don't work, we can't pay those bills. I mean, we aren't broke or anything *now*, but the implication is if I gain any more weight I'll be putting us in the poorhouse."

I can tell she has more to say so I wait.

"So, yeah, I'm fat. That sucks to hear straight to your face, especially when your body is your business."

Now I'm pissed, and it has gone far beyond underarm prickles. "You think you're fat? Cuz some asshole who thinks women should resemble coat hangers told you so?"

Kemina makes this huffing sound. Again, loud enough to carry across the alley.

"Kemi, get real. Do you *really* think you're fat?"

I wait but still no answer.

"So, what you're saying is that all teenage girls and women who look at your jeans advertisements should see a freaking *concave* ass… and that's what they should aspire to having? And guys who check your ads out should be taught to think that women's butts should be flat as pancakes?"

I know she's not ready to answer, but I press on with this argument, which I'm aware could get me tossed from her life as cleanly as she was tossed from the size two photo shoot.

"And that size *four* is in some way revolting?" I'm shooting my mouth off now.

Still silence, except for the sound of the wind.

"And shit, Kemina, if you *were* fat, would it be *really* that big of a deal? *Jeez.* You'd still be you."

At that, she speaks. "Tell me the truth, Justine. Would *you* have looked twice into the window across the alley if I'd been a *fat* girl?"

Honesty is a double-edged sword. I shrug, ashamed at the truth I'm gonna share. "Maybe… but probably not."

Kemina shouts, "Face it—everything in our society is based on what you look like! And the biggest crime of all is being fat because you can supposedly control it."

I nod, and although I accept that she's correct—I probably wouldn't have found myself gawking in her window had she not been so hot—I also know that once I took a good look into her honest eyes, I wouldn't have given a crap about her body's shape.

But would I have made the effort to look into her eyes to begin with, had her body not been so appealing?

"So are you gonna do sit-ups and leg lifts tonight 'til you crash? To burn off your 'excess body fat'?" I sound more sarcastic than I'd intended, and I even make those hated air quotes with my fingers, but I'm pretty mad. I think what I'm really asking her is if she's going to take this criticism of her body by that photographer, and the reinforcement of it by her mother, lying down. "And what about the stuff we discussed at the art museum? You know, how every person's idea of perfect is different? You realized that day that there are *all sorts* of beautiful!"

She ignores my question as she's sort of stuck on what she asked me earlier. "Admit it, Justine—you wouldn't have given me the time of day if I'd resembled one of Picasso's *Two Nudes,* or that sculpture, *The River.* You wouldn't have looked twice if I hadn't been Kemina the Green Vixen of Nightingale Vixen Lingerie status."

It's getting to be a strain to shout across the alley, but I need her to get my point even if it spells the end of whatever it is we've built together. "I'd be lying if I told you otherwise—yeah, your hotness caught my eye. But I'll also admit that I was wrong in judging you by your body, and not by *you*. And that I learned a lot about *myself* by getting to know you and finding out that your personality is even better than your body."

Kemina starts to say something, but then she stops. "I'm cold. I'm going inside."

"Okay." I'm not about to beg and plead. But I *do* say, "I think you're beautiful... and it means more cuz I *know* you."

After a startled look that makes me wonder if anyone has ever told her that she has value beyond her appearance, she turns and leaves.

If she goes back into her room, I can't tell. The light stays off and the curtains remain closed all night.

15

It's weird how you can miss someone who hasn't been a very big part of your life, and who hasn't been around for very long. But I realize, now that Kemina isn't coming to the window anymore, that exchanging signs with her was kinda like the rich fudgy frosting on my life cake. And she just never comes to the window anymore.

Life cake isn't the same without the frosting.

Every night for the past five or so, I could see her in her room, since her new curtains are sheer. I could see her exercising her ass off, pretty much literally, getting weighed and sized by Mama Lopez, who showed up regularly armed with her trusty scale and a tape measure, and sometimes I'd see her studying on her bed. But she hasn't come to the window to exchange signs with me once since the night we spoke on the roof.

I've been distracting myself by watching NBA and WNBA games on my computer, playing as much basketball as I can at the YMCA, and, of course, doing my usual minimal studying I can get by with. The twins have been less of a source of worry since Pam has apparently decided that she wants to play mommy with them. I just hope that she isn't simply trying on the "mommy" role to see if it fits, cuz Jake and Jory are getting attached to her.

At this point, there's only one thing I can think of to do that will help me to stop staring at the window every night like Kemina's semistalker. So I sit at my desk and tear off the cardboard on the back of the sketchbook I've been using to send her messages. Then I scribble down, *If you wanna talk, here's my cell number,* write my number underneath it, and I prop it up in the window…and I leave it there. The ball is now in Kemina's court, so I can stop obsessing over her. In theory.

As I settle back down at my desk, there's a knock on my bedroom door. I get up and open the door, and who I see standing there makes my heart sink to the tips of my high tops. "Hey, Pam. S'up?" Just what I'm freaking *not* in the mood for.

Pam walks right past me into my room before I even have a chance to give the excuse that I'm swamped with homework. Then she sits on the end of my bed like she's been invited. "Good evening, Justine." She hesitates, but I can already tell that tonight's version of Pam is what I'd call purposeful. "The boys, as well as your father and I, missed you at dinner earlier. And at dinner for the last few nights, as well."

"Yeah, well… I figure with you cooking for them… and Dad being home and all, that the two of them are in good hands."

"Your father and I, and a few decent meals, do not make up for your absence. Those boys know you've been eating peanut butter and jelly all by yourself up here instead of sitting with us at the kitchen table." The look she gives me could chip paint, and I feel shamed. "Now, doll, I know something is bothering you because those boys have been your top priority since your mother left, and this indifferent behavior is unlike you."

Is she really gonna try to talk about Mom with me? My stomach churns.

"I, personally, think you are in love."

Oh, so now she's Perceptive Pam? "Nah, Pam, you got that totally wrong."

"Well, maybe you haven't identified it as love, per se, but the look in your eyes tells me you are hurt and distracted and a bit wistful."

I fight the impending nausea.

I am not going to have this conversation with Perfect Pamela Perkins.

"So tell me what his name is."

And I immediately know how to shut her up fast, and how to do it with style. I tilt my head, send her a sarcastic grin, and reply, "It' not a *he*, Pam. It's a *she*."

I have to give her credit. She doesn't grimace even slightly at my confession. "So tell me what *her* name is."

Pam's matter-of-fact reply catches me off guard. I end up answering her. "Um…it's Kemi."

"Kimmy?"

"No, Keh-mee."

Pam smiles. "And this Kemi person, is she a girl at school?"

I shake my head and my eyes are drawn to the window. Pam's gaze follows mine and we're both looking into Kemina's bedroom at the shadowy form exercising behind the sheer curtains.

"Oh, I see." Pam gets up and moves to the window, and when she gets there she lifts my sign to read it and then carefully replaces it. "Have you met this young lady in person?"

I nod. "A couple of times."

"And what is it about her that you like so much?"

From there, whatever restraint I have falls away like it was looking for an excuse to flee. I just start spilling. I tell Pam about how it all started with "sign language" and about meeting up at Naldo's Café, and then I fill her in on my secret-not-lover's identity, the famous Nightingale Green Vixen, Kemina. Which leads to the whole exercising and dieting thing, and finally to Kemi's mother and the paparazzi and our discussion on the roof. I'm basically out of breath when my babbling ends.

Then the most ironic thing happens. Pam pats the bed beside her, so I sit down, and she says, "It sounds like Kemina is trying to be perfect. And achieving perfection is impossible." She purses her little cupid's bow lips and says, "All we can do is try our best."

And Imperfect Pam is right on the money with that assessment. I show her I agree with her by saying, "Kemina doesn't really get it that nobody wants perfection."

"I disagree. Some people really *do* expect perfection. Some people expect it of others... and some people expect it of themselves." She reaches her arm around me, and pulls me toward her like a real mother might do, and I let her. "Before you spoke to me so candidly about how I needed to behave to make things work with the boys and your father, I was trying to be perfect. But it was the wrong kind of perfect."

"The wrong kind?"

"Yes, doll." For some reason, I don't mind it so much when she calls me doll tonight. "I was trying to dress perfectly, to eat selectively, and to sleep sufficiently, so that I always looked my best, and I thought I had to be charming and funny and affectionate—but only with your father." She gestures to her clothes. "And look at me now." I had missed that she is wearing a very casual light pink sweat suit instead of a skirt and a silky top like before. Not *casual* in the same sense as the enormous sweat pants I'm now wearing, but not perfectly tailored either. And instead of being fully made up, she has on a bit of lip gloss and maybe something light on her eyes, but not a lot like before when she always looked made up enough to be going to the opera. "And you know what we had for dinner?"

I shake my head. "Nuh-uh."

"Cheeseburgers and french fries." Her gaze shifts to the side and she blushes as if she's guilty of contributing to the delinquency of minors.

"That's not too gourmet, Pam."

"And do you know what? I let the boys shape the burgers and I didn't even make them wash their hands first." She wrinkles her nose but simultaneously grins so I'm okay with it.

"I guess you aren't exactly perfect anymore."

Pam pushes a few unruly hairs into her ponytail and again fixes her brown eyes on me. "It wasn't easy at first, not doing what I considered to be the perfectly correct thing. You remember when I ate all those cookies, right, doll?"

"You looked like you were gonna toss your cookies—as in, literally."

Pam rubs her belly and smiles uncomfortably. "I rather thought so, as well." Then she stands up. "But since I've relaxed my standards for myself, well, now your father says, 'How could any woman be a more perfect fit for my family?'"

"But are you happy not being the old 'Perfect Pam'?"

This time Pam actually grins. "Oh, yes. I let go of a lot of unimportant standards and I made room for more important ones... like making popsicles. The boys and I are making pineapple-banana-smoothie popsicles. Care to join us?"

I don't even have to think about it. "Sounds like just the study break I need."

Pam and I both glance over at Kemina's window and we can see her shadowy form jogging on her trampoline. "Give Kemina a bit of time to sort out what perfect really means. People can change rather quickly when motivated properly." She winks at me and I follow her from my room.

16

"I've made a decision."

The conversation doesn't start with a "Hello" or "Is this Justine?" or "How are you doing?" And it *sounds* like Kemina, but voices can sound different over the phone, plus I'm walking on a busy New York City street, which doesn't help the whole identifying-the-voice-on-the-phone thing. But I don't recognize the number, so in the likely event it's Kemi, I play along. "You wanna share it with me?"

"Well, that *is* why I called you, Justine." She sounds snippier and more impatient than usual, but at least I'm pretty sure it's Kemi now. On the plus side, she has this certain way of saying my name, almost as if my name is Joust-ine, that I really like, and I really missed. "So fill me in," I say calmly. A big part of me wants to rage at her—"you freaking never came to the window for a week!"—but I don't. I decide to put her needs first, cuz I already know that she must've been struggling hard with whatever decision she's calling to tell me about.

"I'm done starving and sweating and getting on the scale morning, noon, and night." She says it fast, but I manage to catch every word. "I'm done with waking up in the morning and wondering, which diet am I on today?"

"What does this mean for your... uh, your life?" I stop myself before I say, "What does this mean for your career?" because it's her life as a whole that's important, not just her work.

"I'm not sure I much care." I can tell by her tone that she does care, though.

"Seriously?"

Her sigh is audible, even louder than the taxis' beeping horns and the rest of the city noise. I think she knows I caught her in a lie. "It isn't my job I'm so worried about, Justine. It's Mama. I haven't... well, you know."

"You haven't told her that you're gonna live differently?"

"Not yet." Another loud sigh. "But I'm going to." She hesitates a minute, and then adds, "I have to. I'm tired of praying that I get some kind of eating disorder so I won't want to eat anymore."

"Jeez, Kemi. That's pretty awful."

"You're telling me."

As I talk to her, I'm making my way through the busiest part of Times Square on my way to the subway on 42nd Street, after having been birthday present shopping for the twins. And it's getting louder on the street, so it's even harder to hear her.

"Can we talk when I get home? I'm in Times Square so it won't be that long."

"Mama's here tonight, so you can't come over."

"Then you can come over to my apartment. Dad took the boys to a movie."

"Well, you have my number on your phone now, so call when you get close. I'll be waiting."

"Will do."

Her voice softens. "Maybe we can brainstorm ideas of ways I can break the news to Mama—that her Kemina might not be the Baby Vixen anymore."

Kemina is such a paradox. So sure of herself one minute, and then so insecure the next. Sometimes a woman, and other times just a girl. All I know is I want to be the one to help her figure things out. I sprint toward the subway station. People probably think I stole something.

17

She catches me totally off guard. It's like, my mind is all caught up in Kemina and so I miss the huddled mass between our two brownstones.

"Justy."

As soon as I hear the crackly voice and the nickname only one person has ever called me, I know. I freeze with one foot on the bottom step.

"Justy, I've missed you and... I've been clean for twelve days and... things are gonna be different now."

Our conversations always start this way. They have since five weeks after she split and it continues until right now, five years after she took off cuz she "needed a change".

My emotional journey in respect to dealing with my mother's departure went something like this: After I got through the denial and accepted that she was really gone, I moved into my hopeful phase. I used to hope so hard that what she kept telling me was true—that things were gonna be different that time—cuz I loved her, warts and all. But after the first ten fruitless meetings and all of the broken promises and witnessing her body's decline into addiction—well, the hope turned into something close to hate. And after I got over the hatred, which took a while, anger rushed in, and then bitterness, and then another, and yet another negative feeling filled the spot in my heart that used to be filled with love for my mother. Weird thing is, up until this very moment, I thought I'd *finally* achieved apathy. But the righteous fury and undeniable irritation that my mother's mere existence in my life is once again interrupting a moment that really matters is impossible to ignore.

"What are you doing here, Mom?" I know it's blunt and cold and maybe cruel, but ninety-nine per cent of me just doesn't give a crap.

"I missed seeing you and… it's been so long since I visited with you and the boys. It's been since last summer."

I find myself staring at my mother with a brand new sense of revulsion. Half of her front tooth is now a thing of the past, she's dirty to the point of seeming kinda scaly, her hair is tangled beyond the potential benefits of a comb, and her body gives the word skinny a whole new meaning. I've seen her looking bad before—really bad, as a matter of fact—but right now I am embarrassed for her. And more for me. All I can think is that I don't want Kemina to step out of her building and be presented with this street-person mother of mine.

"Mom, you're supposed to call Dad if you wanna see us." I've never said anything like this to her before. Even when I was deep in my hatred phase, I never came even remotely close to rejecting her. But sure as shit, I'm doing it right now, and despite Mom's victim-of-war appearance, she has the presence of mind to be offended. And to show her hurt on her bony-jawed face. Being who I am, her pained expression hurts me right back.

"Oh...well...okay, Justy. I... I just thought...." She lifts herself from the sidewalk, and without another word, hobbles away from me toward I haven't a clue where.

And I stare at her like I've never before seen a homeless person. Cuz seeing her walk away hurts like it always has, and I feel guilty for being appalled by the sight of her, the sound of her, the smell of her, but mostly for being so majorly relieved that she's gone.

"Who was that?" Kemina had somehow snuck up on me as I watched my mother shuffle away in the opposite direction down the sidewalk.

Shit on a freaking shingle!

"Justine, do you *know* that homeless person?"

I turn and look at her. In my romantic mind, her green eyes seem luminous, almost glowing. I shake my head and deliver a smooth lie. "No, she's just some random street person."

"You were talking to her."

"I told her she couldn't stay here."

Kemina's bright eyes cloud over. She's clearly disappointed in me—in the fact that I could be even remotely cruel to someone so helpless. "Why did you say that to her? She wasn't hurting anyone."

Little does Kemina know how much that woman has hurt me. "She scares my little brothers when she sits there."

"Oh."

"I asked her *nicely* to leave." I sound so pathetic, like a sorry excuse for a humanitarian. "My dad told me to ask her to leave when she comes near our building."

"She's just down on her luck, Justine."

I cough a couple of times to hide my surprise. My shock. My guilt. When I recover, I say, "Wanna come in? I have to hide this in my room like ASAP." I show her the Toys-R-Us bag that holds my brothers' Xbox games I picked up for their birthday.

Kemi glances back at her house, and then nods. "I'd love to come in."

I'm actually still shaking a little bit from the shock of that unexpected run-in with Mom when we get to my room.

"You're trembling, Justine." Kemi tosses her long black hair back behind her shoulders and she reaches for me. Despite my desperate need to hide the evidence of my freak-out, I move into her arms. At the moment, my need for comfort and warmth is too powerful to ignore. She holds me kinda tight and I can feel her breasts pressed up against my strapped down chest. I almost don't know how to react to this. My head and my heart are filled with a serious longing that's closely coupled with an unfamiliar sense of everything-is-A-okay-when-I'm-with-Kemina. And when her fingers find my hair and then her thumbs rub my neck—the epicenter of my stress—all I want in the world is to climb inside her. To be a part of her.

"I'm not needy." I declare this softly into her ear for some unknown reason, and then I touch her hair with my fingertips and sniff her neck's sweetness. "Just shakin' cuz I had too much coffee, or something."

"Whatever it is, Justine, it's all right with me." And then she pushes me back, but I cling to her tighter. I'm not ready to let her go. I feel so safe, and I honestly can't remember the last time I felt this way, but still she pushes again and utters, "I only want to kiss you."

Kemina's lips are so soft and so sweet as they press against mine—I'm overwhelmed by the sensation. As her tongue creeps into my mouth, I feel a pulling sensation between my legs that I've only before felt when I was alone. I find myself kinda rhythmically pressing my hips against hers. And a huge part of me wants to be in control here, but I'm lost and I cling to Kemi, and again thrust my hips forward in an effort to find relief. I'm pretty sure I moan right into her open mouth.

"Aaahh, Justine, you're sweet… just like I suspected." And I want to argue that point, insisting that *she* is the sweet one here, but I can't find my voice.

Or maybe we're somehow both sweet. I just can't make sense of it right now.

Before we get too carried away, though, Kemina presses firmly against my belly with both hands, and says in that raspy voice, "It's time for us to talk."

And I'm thankful that she put on the brakes. I have no idea where our intimacy is headed. And the truth is, I'm not yet ready to find out. So, I fake calmness and I take her hand and lead her to my bed where we sit beside each other. But I refuse to let go of her hand, even when she tugs slightly.

After nervously clearing my throat, like maybe five times in a row, I ask, "What made you decide to give up on all of the dieting and exercising?"

And just like that, the mood in my bedroom changes dramatically, and it feels like the temperature drops twenty-five degrees. Suddenly, Kemina is serious and almost businesslike. As usual, she thinks for a few minutes before she replies. I can't help but study Kemi as she gazes at her hands that are folded in her lap. I take in her full lips and even fuller dark hair that falls loose and a bit wild over her shoulders, and those emerald-green eyes that look like they're outlined with thick smudges of charcoal. I wonder if I'm seeing "perfect" when I look at her because she's so beautiful or because she's fast becoming mine.

"Mostly, it's because of something *you* said."

I search my memory to recall exactly what we'd talked about on the roof that windy night.

"You said, but not exactly in these words, that *I'm* part of the conspiracy."

I know I look shocked because I feel shocked—I don't remember accusing her of anything close to that.

She reaches over and squeezes my hand. "*I'm* part of modern society's plan to make us all live up to a *certain* standard of beauty. A standard of so-called perfection that is nearly impossible to attain, and unreasonable to expect of people."

"You mean, how I said that your jeans advertisements are teaching girls that a good ass is a concave one?"

She smiles. "Yes. That was what got me thinking. Women feel like less if they aren't a size two, and men are trained to think the same way."

"So what are you gonna do?"

Kemina stands up, and I see in her a strength I've never before noticed. "Well, to start with, I have to tell Mama I'm getting off the dieting merry-go-round. And for me, that's the hardest part of this whole thing."

I'm suddenly pissed off that the person who should be Kemi's number one supporter is her number one fear factor. But I manage to breathe through the anger without exploding.

"And once I do that, I'm going to set up a meeting with the guy I deal with at Vixen Lingerie. His name is Grant Pederson, and he's been very nice to work with to this point."

"That was when you were following all the rules," I remind her.

Ignoring what I said, Kemina starts to pace back and forth in front of my bed. "I just have so many ideas, Justine, of how *I* can be the one to make some important changes. I feel like I'm in the right position to do this."

"How do you mean?"

"Think of it: a fashion model known for body perfection standing up for body acceptance. There is absolutely no one better to do this." Her elated expression shows that she is incredibly inspired by the whole idea. "But first...."

"You've gotta talk to your mom."

The balloon metaphorically pops and Kemina hunches over a bit, all of the air fizzling out of her fairly swiftly.

"I know you can do it." I believe she can talk to her mother and make the woman see, because mothers deserve a chance. And I think she needs to hear me say this.

Then an image of my own mother, slumped over, filthy and weary, shuffling alone down the sidewalk, flashes in front of my eyes. I blink quickly to drive the image away. I remind myself that this is not about me.

18

"Your mother wants to see you and the boys."

Pam is sitting beside Dad on the living room couch, holding his hand like it's some kind of a prize. Lately, she's here more often than she's not, and strangely, I don't mind too much. I try to read her expression—to figure out if she's jealous that our *real* mother is trying to insert herself into a space that Pam has recently occupied—but I get nothing. Her expression is blank, her nose isn't wrinkled, and she's looking up at me as if she's serene... in the face of my misery.

"It's just gonna be the same old thing all over again, and you know it, Dad."

"Laura says she's making a real effort to stay off all of the...substances." I can't tell if he wants me to see her or not.

"But I haven't mentioned it to the boys yet, as I wanted to get your feelings on this first."

I nod at him, glad of that. "I don't kno-o-ow," I whine. This is the first time I have ever *not* jumped at the chance to see my mother. Cuz I know, I know—hope endures, and Mom said "this time is gonna be different" and maybe she's telling the truth.

But things with her never seem to change.

Pam stands up and steps beside me. "She's made mistakes. She's not perfect—none of us are. Right, Wally?" She bats her eyelashes at Dad and he drinks it in like sweet apple cider.

I'm instantly pissed. *Who the hell is Peacemaker Pam to suggest I go easy on this woman who has strapped me with the burden my brothers' rejection and my father's loneliness and a shit ton of my own pain, too?* "I'd say she's about as far from perfect as you can get."

"Look, doll." The term "doll" irritates the crap out of me at the moment—like nails on a chalkboard. "I'm not suggesting that you see her for *her* benefit. I'm only thinking of you."

Of me? Huh? "Whatever." I know it's rude, but I say it anyway.

Dad stands up and puts himself between us, as if I'm infected with some nasty rudeness disease that he doesn't want his

Precious Pammy to catch. "Just think about it and let me know, okay, Justine?"

I nod as I head for the stairs. "I grabbed pizza with the guys tonight after basketball. Don't expect me at dinner."

I just know that Dad and Pam are looking at each other with worried eyes and shaking their heads.

When I get to my room, I immediately look into Kemi's window. Today is the day she planned to inform her mother that she was going to, as she calls it, "be normal" with food and exercise. The light's on and the curtains are open, but she's not in there, so I figure she's telling her mom right now.

I'm feeling all kinds of unsettled. Between her mom and my mom and my brand new sort-of-mom, I'm not at all on my game. So I leave the lights off and lie on my bed and stare at the ceiling, every once in a while glancing to the side to see if Kemi is stretched out on her bed, too.

It sounds so freaky, but I sense when she's about to enter her bedroom. So I'm already looking when she runs in and *tries* to slam her door with no lock. I wonder, *what good is that gonna do? If your mom wants to come in, she'll come right on in!*

Mrs. Lopez pushes the door open, causing her daughter to stumble backward. When Kemi stands back up, her mother slaps her hard across the face. Kemina reaches for her right cheek and her mother takes that opportunity to slap her with equal force across her left cheek.

I'm instantly on my feet, my armpits prickling uncomfortably with my agitation, and I start scrambling around the bedroom in search of my phone.

This is crazy! This is abuse! Kemina!

I can feel that my eyes are wet and dripping, although I don't think I'm actually crying. I'm just so furious! I stop scrambling around long enough to see if Mrs. Lopez further attacks her daughter, but she doesn't. She just folds her arms over her chest, purses her lips, and then stares at Kemina. When Kemi's mom finally unfolds her arms, she points to the trampoline and nods once, as if a decision has been made. I watch to see if Kemina will obediently step up on the trampoline, but she doesn't. She hunches over and focuses her gaze on the floor, and I know that she's closing herself off from the world. *But she doesn't get on the trampoline.* After shooting Kemi a final pissed-off glare, Mrs. Lopez turns and leaves.

Suddenly, I just need to hear Kemi's voice and for her to hear mine. All I can think to do is call her. I seriously doubt that she's gonna answer her phone. But when she hears it ring, she walks over to her bureau, picks up her phone, looks at it, and answers. "Hello?"

"Kemi!"

"It didn't go so well with Mama." She sounds worn out. "Did you see?"

"It would've been hard to miss. You okay? Want me to come over? She can't hit you like that, you know! You're not a little kid…. I-I don't want her to touch you again!" I'm rambling.

"No." I hear one of those loud sighs. "Don't come over… it'll only make things worse."

"Please Kemi, please… I wanna see you. Wanna make sure you're okay…." Not too long ago I'd told myself that I wasn't the type to beg and plead. And all of a sudden, I'm *exactly* that type.

"Okay… okay, Justine. But just don't ring the buzzer. I'll come down in ten minutes or so and let you in." She sounds so defeated and I know I don't want to be in any way responsible for that tone in her voice.

I force myself to say, "Only if you want me to. I won't come over if you think it's better that I stay away."

Kemina deserves free choice, just like I do.

"I really want to see you," she says. "But I don't want Mama to know."

"Wanna come here?"

"No... no, it'll be better if I can sneak you in here."

"Ten minutes?"

"Just wait for me downstairs."

It isn't the best-laid plan, and it doesn't work, which shouldn't have surprised me even slightly. Just as we're sneaking up the stairs, Mrs. Lopez comes out of the kitchen.

"What on God's green earth do you think you are doing, Kemina?" We jolt around to gawk at her, both of us almost falling down the stairs in the process. "Oh, other than ruining your life, and mine in the process."

Kemina finds her balance and yanks her hand from mine. "I'm having a friend over. It's not an unheard of thing for a teenager to do." Her voice sounds surprisingly strong, maybe even a bit defiant.

"Hi, Ms. Lopez," I offer weakly. Kemi's mother doesn't even glance at me; her eyes are fixed on her daughter. I'm an unimportant incidental.

"You may want to let yourself go and become a fat dyke, Kemina, and that is all well and good. But over my dead body will it happen while you are under contract with Nightingale."

"It's *my* contract, Mama. It's *my* concern." Her voice is quiet now, even trembling a little bit. All traces of defiance are suddenly gone. It really didn't take too much effort on the woman's part to have Kemi cowering.

"Get down here." The look in Mrs. Lopez's eyes tells me that she means business. Kemina steps down the stairs and stands in front of her mother. No longer is she in any way bold, instead she looks afraid, which kills me. I want to protect her somehow, but I'm scared that my efforts will just make everything worse. "Do I have to remind you that I gave up my work as a legal secretary to manage your career? I've devoted my entire life to you, young lady. And you are throwing it all away so you can carpet munch this... this butch."

Heat rushes to my face. The sexual inference coming from *somebody's mother* is just too much for me. I'm really new at this—at thinking about sexual things and at *being* a sexual person. And although my deepest wish is to help Kemina, I wanna escape.

Her mother points at me, her face a mask of revulsion. "My God, Kemina, *it looks* like a boy... Can't you just go out and find some femme Justin Bieber-wanna-be who is *actually male* to fuck?"

Kemina turns to me. "I'm sorry."

I can't meet her eyes. I just shrug and study the beneath my feet. I still want to help, but at the moment I'm pretty much trapped inside my own head. Cuz all of a sudden, I'm an "it"…a butch…a dyke. A carpet muncher. Yeah, I've always been a tomboy but now it isn't just about how I express my gender—now it's about my sexuality.

"I… I'll stay if you want me to, Kemi." I know she can hear the pleading sound in my voice that she please, *please,* just let me leave.

"You will get your hairy lesbian ass out of this house right now!"

"I'm sorry," Kemi says again.

"I… I'm sorry too, Kemina." I trip down the stairs and head toward the door at the end of the hall. But before I open it, I turn back to Kemi. "Come with me." I extend my hand toward her.

Our gazes meet and hold, and in this exchange, there is so much passion.

I don't have a clue why, but something I learned in Sign Language Club during middle school pops into my head. So I extend one arm so that my palm is flat and I place my other fist on top of it, with my thumb sticking up. "This means help." Kemi studies my hands and makes the gesture, as if practicing.

"Out!" Mrs. Lopez bellows in my direction, still refusing to look at me.

"I'll call you, Justine."

"I'll be waiting."

I lie in bed and stare across the alley into Kemi's lit up bedroom, but I'm not rewarded with the sight of my girl.

My girl. Am I her girl, too?

All night I've waited for her phone call, but I've waited for nothing. She doesn't call. I find myself praying to a God I don't know—cuz I'm desperate and I'll take any help I can get right now. I feel so helpless, and worse, I feel like I abandoned Kemina. I left her alone in the lion's den cuz I was having trouble accepting the grittier aspects of my sexuality.

At around midnight Kemina returns to her bedroom. Frantically, I search her face for signs of having been punched or scratched or slapped. But all I see are swollen eyes from too many tears. I experience a strange sense of relief combined with fury.

She comes right to the window, stopping only to grab a notebook and marker. When she gets to the window, she bends down a little and writes, and then she presses the message against the glass.

She took my phone, so I couldn't call you.

I kneel on the edge of my bed and nod my understanding.

I spent the night listening to her rant about how I'm not allowed to be a fat lesbian until I'm at least thirty.

She sends me that crooked smile and after I smile back, I roll my eyes. Then I write on the sketchpad.

As if it's possible to choose your sexuality.

She writes again.

I nodded a lot and cried, too. Mama thinks she's won. But nothing has changed.

I don't know what to write in response to that. I can't imagine what it must feel like to go up against her freaking scary-ass mother.

I'm going to set up an appointment with Grant Pederson from Nightingale. Once I do that, I'll know where I stand with my contract.

How soon can you talk to him?

All things considered, it looks like Kemi is in pretty decent shape. I want her answer to be, "tonight—I can talk to Grant tonight and we'll get everything settled." But I know this is wishful thinking.

Not for the next few days. I have a shoot for a new brand of jeans (if I fit into them-LOL) in Central Park that is going to keep me busy. And very cold. Brrr.

I frown but at the same time I realize that this is her job and she needs to set her priorities as she sees fit.

It's a shoot with guys. There will be a lot of physical contact between us.

I'm not happy about her getting pawed by hunky model-dudes, but I'm also in no position to tell Kemi what she can and can't do. That's been her mother's job. And what I want most is for it to be no one's job but Kemina's.

But I'm thinking that since you're my girlfriend, our relationship is what matters. Not what I do while I'm modeling, because it's not real.

Girlfriend. She wrote the word girlfriend.

I smile.

Justine—what we have together is real.

I scribble down my agreement.

It sure is.

I won't be around 'til the day after tomorrow. And probably not until after dinnertime.

And you don't have your phone. So we can't talk.

Now Kemina frowns, and I suspect she's gonna miss me, which feels pretty good.

I'll try to get my phone back. But if I can't, I'll send you a message on a sign as soon as I return.

We look at each other for a minute. Her eyes are hungry, and I know it's for me, especially since she's been eating like a human being, not a rabbit, lately. I think the expression in my eyes is probably much the same.

Justine, go to sleep with your bedside lamp on. So I can see you if I wake up in the night.

I point to her and mouth the words, "You do it too."

She nods and smiles. Then we both get ready for bed.

I write a final message on the back of a paper plate I swipe from the trash, and I leave it on the windowsill.

Sleep well, my girl. ☺

Lying on our sides with our heads propped on our pillows and the lamps beside our beds lit, we stare into each other's eyes until we fall asleep.

19

"You played like Candace Parker today—what's up with that, Bieber?" Bart never knows when to call it quits with the Justin Bieber crap.

"Bite me." A suitable response, I figure, given the circumstances.

"Can't a dude give another dude a compliment without gettin' his head bitten off?"

"That's what the female praying mantis does to the male after they get it on. She bites his head right off." Joey can always be counted on to be there to offer senseless commentary to distract us from our bickering. "At least, that's what I heard."

"So what's up with your Olympic performance at the Y?" Bart isn't going to let it drop. He wants to know what inspired my stellar performance on the court—it seems I couldn't miss a shot.

I want to tell them that the reason I'm unstoppable is cuz I've got a girl now—a girl who's smart and strong and brave and sweet and so many more things. But at the same time, I'm kinda freaked about letting them know I like girls. I mean, these guys know I *act* a lot like a guy, but they also know I'm *not* a guy. At least not where it really seems to count to them, which happens to be between my legs. All they know is we head to different locker rooms after we scrimmage. So, in theory, I'm supposed to be looking at guys *that way*, not at girls like me.

But like I said, Kemina's brave, and she's owning up to *her* truth—she's gonna stop starving herself so she can live up to somebody else's idea of perfect—and it could be at the cost of her job and maybe even her mother. Out of respect for her, I decide to put my truth out there, too. I'm risking far less than she is.

"I got a girl—that's why I'm unstoppable!" Their eyes go wide, but I don't give them a chance to ask questions. I turn around and run out the door of the YMCA and shout back at them when they get to the street, "Maybe if you guys got yourselves girlfriends you'd play more like LeBron James."

"Hey, wait up!"

"We want details, Laraby!"

"All the dirty ones!"

There's plenty of time for details. I have this gut feeling that Kemina and I are only just beginning.

Tonight I'm feeling more than a little bit like a stalker.

I blew off getting food with the guys and rushed home from the Y, took a quick walk-through shower, and now I'm eating a homemade-by-Pam-and-the-boys ham and cheese Panini, while planted on my bed and watching, in a hawklike fashion, for Kemina's return. Her curtains are halfway closed, but I can still see inside her room pretty well, so I'll know when she gets in. But it's almost eight, and I expected her back a few hours ago. A feeling of anxiety tugs at my heart, and I try to dismiss it with another huge bite of my sandwich, but even the taste of too much Grey Poupon doesn't do much to distract me.

Finally the light goes on across the alley. Kemina walks into her bedroom and closes the door, slung over her shoulder is a large orange duffle bag that she drops onto the floor beside the bed. She immediately goes to her "starvation rations" drawer and pulls it open, even before looking across the alley at me, and I figure she must be basically ravenous. If her mother was with her on the photo shoot, she probably forced Kemi to eat nothing but lettuce for the past two days.

She's bent over grabbing the snack of her choice when the bedroom door opens again, and I think, *shit, caught with her hand in the cookie jar,* or drawer, in this case. But it isn't her mother who enters the room. It's this uber-cocky, really good-looking dude. And when I say good-looking, I mean that I can tell he's also a model.

My view is obstructed slightly by the curtains, but I quickly get the general idea of what's going down. When she stands back up, he moves right behind her and puts his arms around her waist. Immediately she tries to pull away, but his hands must be locked together on her belly, and he won't let go. He then stuffs his face into the hollow of her neck, which is fully exposed because her hair is tied up in one of those high ponytails. And from what I can see, she doesn't like it one bit, which she makes abundantly clear.

I'm freaking out at this point. I reach for my phone and I dial her number and look through the window to see if they react to the ringing phone, but neither one of them seems to hear it. Only then do I remember that Kemina's mom has her phone. But as I sit there listening to my call get sent to Kemi's voicemail, he turns her around by her shoulders and mouth-dives for her lips. Kemi is pushing against his chest and turning her head back and forth to avoid the kiss, but these things do not deter him slightly.

And then I see it. Her hands reach behind his back and she makes the sign I taught her for "help." That's all it takes to get me moving.

I race down the stairs and right past my family as they play M&M Monopoly in the living room. Dad and Pam jump to their feet as I run past, but I don't take time to explain. I run down our building's stairs and over to Kemi's brownstone, and within a split second I'm alternately pounding on the lobby door and pressing the buzzer.

After what seems like fifteen minutes but is probably only thirty seconds, a calm and smug Mrs. Lopez comes to the entryway door. She folds her arms across her chest and just looks at me through it, like, *what are you gonna do about this, dyke?* But I'm not stupid and I lift up my phone and shout pretty loud, "Let me in or I'll call 911."

She gets my meaning, and after a brief hesitation and the pursing of her lips, she opens the door. At this point, I can hear my family outside on the sidewalk calling my name and asking what's going on. Still, I don't slow down to answer them. I fly up the stairs and I'm in Kemina's bedroom in no time at all.

"Let her go!"

Mr. Eye-Candy-but-still-an-asshole is pretty much shocked by the interruption. He takes a step back from Kemina and holds his hands up like he didn't even touch her, in the innocent manner of a basketball player who just fouled another guy on the court. "I'm not doin' nothin' wrong...." he says, but I saw the evidence of what he did with my own eyes.

I step past him to Kemina, who's already in closed-off-to-the-world mode, hunched over and staring at the floor. "Hey, you okay, Kemi? I got here as fast as I could."

She nods but doesn't lift her head.

"Look here, dude, Kemina's mom told me she has it bad for me, but she likes to play hard to get. So after I drove them two home from the shoot, Mrs. L said I oughta come up here and show her what a real man is." For some reason he's directing this explanation to me. "I didn't know she had a boyfriend or nothin'."

Kemina slowly raises her head as his words sink in—her mother set her up. And when her chin lifts a bit more, and I can see her eyes, in them I see defiance. Which is all well and good and shit, but I'm pretty much chomping at the bit to take a swing at the asshole, and so I step forward and grab onto his shirt with that very intention. "The girl was freaking pushing you away, jackass! *No means no*, ever heard of that?" And I shake him as hard as I can.

His chin rattles a bit, and instead of asking me how I know what went down in her bedroom, he again insists, "Her mother said she was like super into me!" He turns to Kemi. "Your mom *told me* you want me!" He grabs his crotch to further demonstrate his meaning.

I don't feel bad for the guy even slightly cuz he was taking from Kemi what wasn't offered to him, but that little tidbit of information really sucks. Apparently now, the only thing Kemina wants is for him to be out of her sight. "Just get out of here, Kyle," she says in a monotone. But he continues to stand there staring and so I'm compelled to shake him again. "You don't need to hit him, Justine. Kyle is leaving. *Right, Kyle?*"

I can identify the very moment pretty-boy-Kyle realizes that he's been getting tossed around like a ragdoll by a girl. He shakes his head a few times, as if he's doing some kind of a reality check, and then he pulls away from me. "So the rumors are true, Kemina. You *are* a lesbo." He turns around and walks out.

Kemina doesn't rush into my arms as if she's some kind of damsel in distress and I'm her Prince Charming. And yeah, maybe I wish she would—maybe I want her to. In fact, she takes a step *away* from me, and mutters, "Mama… My own mother set me up."

You can count on Justine Laraby to say something stupid at the critical moment. "I saw the sign. You made the help sign… and I saw it."

When Kemi turns to me, she doesn't smile, but strangely her eyes are now free of the dark shadows I've come to expect. "Yes, and I knew you'd see it."

I nod, sort of acknowledging that I was peeping into her window, more or less all night.

"Can I stay at your house—until I sort this out?"

"Uh…sure. Not a problem."

She bends down and picks up her duffle bag. "I have almost everything I need in here."

I reach over and take the bag from her, and then sling it over my shoulder. She goes to her closet and pulls out a few more things she needs and folds them over her arm. "Okay, I'm ready to go."

There's a small crowd waiting for us when we get to the steps outside Kemi's brownstone. Dad and Pam are trying to keep the boys from coming inside to find me, Mrs. Lopez is out there, a phone pressed against her ear and yapping angrily, and it seems a fortunate member of the paparazzi, who is probably thanking his lucky stars for being in the right place at the right time tonight, is on the sidewalk snapping pictures.

Because of the presence of the lone photographer, Kemina seems to regain that sense of regal confidence she shows to the public. She straightens her back and lifts her chin. I lead her over to my family.

"Dad, Pam... this is my...um...my girlfriend, Kemina Lopez." I speak quietly, but that paparazzi guy probably has some kind of a zoom microphone attached to his zoom camera.

Dad does his best to hide his shock—not that I have a *girlfriend*, I don't think, but that my girlfriend is a famous underwear model. I can't blame him—it still comes as something of a surprise to me.

"So... a girlfriend? Her name's Kemina, you said?" He says, thinking he's coy.

Come on Dad, everybody knows who she is.

"Yeah, Kemina. And she needs a place to stay. Is it okay if she stays on the couch in the office 'til she works out a couple of things with her... mother?" I want to say "asshole business manager" because that woman has not earned the right to be referred to as a mother.

Mrs. Lopez is at this point pretty much screaming into the phone. I seriously pity the person on the other end, but at the same time I'm glad it's not Kemi. Speaking of Kemi, she passes me the clothing that is hanging over her arm, and steps back over to her mother, clearly wishing to talk. Mrs. Lopez doesn't even acknowledge her.

"Is she an adult... you know, is she eighteen years old?" My dad is being cautious and I can't blame him.

"She turned eighteen in the fall."

"Then I can't see why she shouldn't stay with us for a few days." His eyes are wide, unsure of what to make of this whole scene.

The boys start to whine, with Jory in the lead. "We gotta finish our game, I was just about to win."

"You were not—I'm the one who owns the most M&M ads."

"Yeah maybe, but I got more brown hotels than anybody else."

Pam decides to end their bickering. "Let's get back to our game, boys. When we are finished, I'll make up the pullout couch in the office for Kemina."

The boys run back to our building, leaving Dad and me gawking at each other. "You better get back there, too, Dad. The boys are super into their game and you're part of it."

"If you need me here, Justine, this is where I need to be."

I shake my head. "Nah. I'm all set." We both glance at Kemina. "We'll come over as soon as she tells her mother what's up."

Dad eyes travel from Kemi to her mother to me. He tilts his head and says quietly, "You don't have a lot of reasons to be a big fan of mothers, do you?"

I shrug.

"Mothers aren't all... like the ones you've seen close up. Some are wonderful." His voice breaks on the "der" syllable.

I'm less than convinced by his claim. "Excuse me if I have my doubts."

He nods and grabs kind of awkwardly at my hand. "You have a very beautiful girlfriend, Jussy."

I smile and then I correct him. "Maybe so. But what I like about her isn't just the stuff you can see. You get me?" I really need him to get what I'm trying to say. "Her coolness is more on the inside."

Nodding again, Dad lets go of my hand and turns toward our apartment building, but looks back once more at Kemi and her mom, who are currently engaged in some kind of a silent, staring, hands-on-hips standoff. "Good luck," he says to no one in particular.

"We're gonna need it," I hear myself mumble. Dad turns back and leans toward me, slips the duffle bag off my shoulder and pulls Kemi's clothes from my hand, and then makes his exit. I turn my full attention to my girl, who is now being videotaped by another onlooker's phone.

"Mama, I'm going to be staying with my friend, Justine, next door. Until I sort a few things out."

Grizzly Mama seems to subscribe to the notion that bad publicity is better than no publicity. "You are going to live with that nasty bull dyke?"

Not surprisingly, I've never been referred to as that before. And frankly, I'm kinda stunned. At that moment, the photographer takes the opportunity to shoot a picture of me, the slack-jawed "bull dyke."

"I'm staying with my friend Justine. And leave her out of this."

"*This*? This what?"

"What you set me up for! With Kyle." I can tell Kemina is struggling to maintain her self-control. "I'm not going to discuss this with you out here on the street. I'll be in touch."

Mrs. Lopez takes a step back. The volume of her voice raises a decibel or three. "So this is how you thank me? I gave up my career—my entire life—to make you a success. And this is how you repay me?"

I step over to Kemi and place my hand on her forearm. "I think it's time to go."

Kemina is staring at her mother, a pissed-off scowl on her face, and she somehow still looks pretty. After a couple of seconds, she nods and grabs onto my hand. "Yeah...you're right."

No sooner do we turn and start to walk next door, than Kemina is suddenly dragged to the ground. It takes a second for it to register in my brain: Kemina's mother has tackled her. I only have to turn my head slightly to see them struggling on the sidewalk beside me. Meanwhile, the camera dude is practically moaning with a sort of preorgasmic excitement, as he's certainly seeing the dollar bills he can get for these candid pictures before his eyes rather than Kemina's misfortune. The cell phone videomaker is busy encouraging Mrs. Lopez, "Give it to her good, lady!"

I bend down with the intention of separating them, and see that Kemina's mother has latched her fists into her daughter's hair—one at the scalp and the other onto her ponytail. Kemi's neck is twisted at an odd angle due to her mother's brutal hair-yanking, and on her face are three long fingernail scratches across her right cheekbone. The marks are deep and bleeding.

"Don't think you can just walk away from me, Kemina!" Her voice sounds scary—like she's possessed.

"Let go o' her, ma'am!" I yell and then I grab the lady's wrists and squeeze as hard as I can, forcing Mrs. Lopez to release Kemi's hair. I shout, "Run!" Kemi doesn't need to be told twice and she takes off. I push Kemi's mom gently back so she's flat on the ground and I take the opportunity to bolt. But I can't help it—when I get to the steps of my brownstone, I call back, "You are one crazy-ass bitch!"

Probably not such a good idea.

And there I am on You Tube and *The Gossip Rag—See It Here First,* and *Soulja Boi Dot Com* in all of my stereotypical, pissed-off lesbian glory. My Boston Red Sox cap turned backwards on my Justin Bieber hair, a Tracy Chapman "Matters of the Heart" T-shirt hanging out over my incredibly baggy sweatpants, unlaced high tops to finish the picture, and pointing my finger ruthlessly at an apparently frail older woman who is stretched out helplessly on the ground. "You are one crazy-ass bleeeeep!"

The texts from kids at school, not to mention from the guys I hang with, start pouring in and…. And I could really have lived without this drama.

Thankfully the boys have gone to bed, but Dad, Pam, and Kemi are huddled around my open laptop and me, checking out the damage to my reputation.

"Think Justine will be on the eleven o'clock news?" Pam asks Kemi with wide-eyed innocence.

I shudder at the thought.

"I doubt it," Kemina replies as if this is a daily occurrence in life, which, for her, it probably is. "But I'm betting it will be on some of the late night entertainment shows."

"I'm not going to school tomorrow." That's all I can think of to say.

Dad stands up and takes Pam by the hand. "We're gonna head upstairs. Kemina, you know where the guest room is, and we keep towels in the linen closet in the hallway." Before heading to bed with his girlfriend, he sends me this meaningful look, which

I suppose suggests that I'm not allowed to go to bed with *my* girlfriend.

I shrug, but he keeps on looking at me *that* way, so I nod.

"Judging from your dad's behavior, I take it I'm your first girlfriend?" Kemi asks when they leave the room.

I shrug again, but I admit the truth. "Yeah." I want to know if I'm Kemina's first girlfriend, but I don't ask. She doesn't offer.

"Your parents are really nice."

It hits me that she has just referred to Pam as my mom. And I want so badly to simply say, "Thanks, they are really cool," but again I go with honesty. "Pam's not my mother. She's Dad's girlfriend."

"Well, she seems really into you and your brothers."

"And my dad."

Kemina chuckles. "Well, of course, isn't that a given? Anyway, where's your *real* mom?"

My girlfriend hasn't exactly been a bubbling fountain of openness with me, but I decide that two don't have to play that game. After all, I've been included in a lot of her life's most private drama, even if it wasn't by invitation. So I spill. "Remember that street person who was sitting on the sidewalk between our buildings?"

That's all I need to say about my *real* mother. "Oh, I see." Kemi gets the picture really fast. "Well, don't we both have serious mommy issues?" She laughs, but I can't make myself join in.

There's a long moment of quiet before Kemina scoots down to my end of the sofa. She drapes an arm over the back of the couch and I can't help but stare at it. ""Hey, I feel your pain," she murmurs in my ear. "Want to forget about our problems for a while?"

When I look back at her, she has the same expression in her eyes as the poster-girl Kemina. I wonder if that look is real or part of some kind of an act to get me going. "What did you have in mind?" My voice trembles.

"This." And then she's kissing me, and I'm overwhelmed by her scent and her softness and all of the pretty hair that she's let fall over her shoulders.

I reach up and touch the silkiness of it as her lips toy with mine in what I take as an invitation. Then a sudden urge to be the bold one overtakes me, and I make what I guess you'd call my move. I lean forward and sort of push her down on her back on the couch, my hand sliding beneath her head before it lands. And I take over this kiss like I actually know what I'm doing. Being on top of her, looking down into her eyes each time we stop to take a breath, feels so right to me. Like I'm supposed to be the one doing the starting and stopping of the kissing. And my fingers tingle… I have to hold myself back from reaching up underneath her flowing top and touching the bare skin I know is beneath it. I'm pretty sure she'd let me touch her if I tried, but then I really don't know if I'd want her to reciprocate it. In fact, the thought of her pretty hands on my chest makes me grit my teeth, and I need to figure out why before I go there with her. I quickly decide that when it's the right moment to be more intimate with Kemi, I'll somehow know it, cuz all my doubts will be gone.

But I don't have to worry about whether or not to reach for her breasts very long because she starts pushing up on my chest, and when I raise my lips from hers to see what she wants, she says, "Let's talk."

I'm secretly relieved by this change in direction, but I try not to show it. I just lean back against the corner of the couch like I'm completely cool with what's going on, and Kemi curls up right beside me. I'm still turned on to the max, and more than anything, I hope that she is too. But also I'm somehow satisfied cuz what went down with us is fine for now. And finally, uber-cool me is ready to speak. "So what's on your mind?"

"Besides the fact that you're adorable?" She's flirting and I like it.

"Yeah, besides that." I grin at her and she touches my chin very lightly with her thumb.

Then she drops her hand to her lap and says, "Well, this is like the first time I've ever gone up against Mama." She thinks for a second, and then adds, "In any way that actually matters." Her voice sounds kind of wonder-filled when finally she admits, "I've always been so scared of doing just this. I could never say, 'No, Mama, I don't want to do it that way'."

"So it was like you had a hard time setting boundaries with her?"

Kemi looks shocked, almost like no one ever before has understood this. "I usually just do everything I can to avoid the drama—you know, I can never win with her."

"So how do you feel now that you *are* doing it? You defied her tonight, Kemi."

"Much better than I thought I would. Strange, huh?"

"Maybe standing up to her has been a long time coming."

"Uh-huh. I think it has, and I'm *so* ready for a change. I've been ready for a long time now, but I've never been able to see myself as I really am. I guess a part of me always believed everything she said—I was fat, unlikeable, and not too smart."

I'm disturbed by what Kemina's mother said about her, and to her, but the selfish part of me is focused on something else. "What do you mean—a change?" I hope she doesn't hear the insecurity that has crept into my voice. My own mother said she "needed a change" when she took off and never came back.

"I want to step back from Mama and see myself clearly for the first time. And I want to do what *I* want to do with my life, not what she makes me feel like I *have* to do."

"And what is that? What do you want to do?" I hope I don't sound needy.

Kemi doesn't answer for a long time. When she does, it sounds wistful. "I want to do what's right for women and for teenage girls, and, you know, for me. I want to make a statement, as a fashion model, about how you can love and accept yourself just as you are. All of us are beautiful, right?" The lights are dim in the living room, but I can still see that Kemi's blushing. I don't think she's ever said so much to me all at once, especially not about her hopes and dreams. "I know it sounds stupid. I don't know what I'm thinking—as if *I* can actually make a change. It's just I've thought a lot about this…and I have all of these ideas…and…."

I reach up and touch her face, just beneath the three scratch marks that are all shiny cuz Pam smeared them with some ointment she says stops infection. "It's not stupid. Not at all. Tell me more." The look she gives me is curious, and I can tell she's wondering if she can really trust me. I don't think she's been given much opportunity to trust anybody in the past.

I must be doing something right, though, cuz Kemi and I talk about the ways she wants to change the world until the early hours of the morning when our eyes are drooping and every other word is spoken through a yawn. Then we drag ourselves up the stairs, Kemi to the couch in the office on the second floor, and me one more flight up to my bedroom. As I drift off to sleep, I glance across the alley into Kemi's bedroom, expecting nothing but darkness. But what I see surprises me. Instead of staring into total darkness, by the dim light of the bedside lamp, I see Mrs. Lopez fast asleep in Kemina's bed.

20

I end up going to school and I wish I hadn't. It seems that lots of kids watch late night entertainment shows, and I'm now known as an "abuser of middle-aged women." There are also no shortage of curious looks that ask without words, "What were you doing with the one and only Kemina?" But everybody's obsession with me wears off as the day wears on.

I take a cab home from school today so I can answer texts, but the only texts I actually respond to are the ones from my guy friends. First off, I tell them no b-ball for me today, as I have to get right home to *my girlfriend* (fist pump!) who is staying at my apartment. And, by the way, did I mention I have *a girlfriend*? Her name is Kemina and we are tight (double fist pump!) They have a million questions, and I do my best to answer them in a very general but noninsulting manner, as I'm not sure how much Kemi wants me to tell them about her.

I run up the stairs when I get home and let myself into the building. "Kemi? You here?" I shout as I enter the living room, but I get no response. I run up a flight and check the office. The bed is made and her towel is hanging on the doorknob. But no girlfriend.

So I charge up one more flight and go into my room. On a fresh new page in my sketchpad, is a note.

I went to meet Grant Pederson. We are going to discuss my future at Nightingale. I'll be back after dinner.

My belly tightens and I'm truthfully not sure why. A bunch of things run through my mind—would Grant try to convince Kemi to apologize to her mother, commit to dropping the ten pounds she's recently gained, and head for the treadmill at her gym, so that she can continue on with her Vixen Lingerie promotion? Would he yell at her and insult her and then fire her, making her feel like she's somehow less than perfect? Would he accept Kemina's decision and then regrettably release her from her contract?

I have no idea how the meeting will go. I just hope she stands her ground, but for eighteen years she's been taught that, in terms of her body size, less is more, so I realize it'll take a lot of strength on her part to stick to her new path. And I don't exactly know Kemina inside and out. I'm not certain how she'll react.

We eat dinner as a family, and now it seems that the family includes Perpetually Present Pam. I'm not knocking the situation, or her—I'm just making an honest observation. Tonight, Pam and the boys cook a rice and vegetable stir-fry, and as far as I can hear from my seat in the living room, they create the healthy meal while orally reviewing vocabulary for the middle school spelling bee later this week. Pam is a perfect mother, it seems, and I shake my head, wondering how she went from "keep your distance, boys" to "I'm here for you, Jake and Jory" in such a short time period. But who am I to question her big transformation? Apparently, it's working for everybody involved.

I clean up from dinner alone, seeing as the boys and Pam cooked, and am only interrupted once when Dad comes in to remind me that Mom still wants to see us. Apparently she got in touch with Dad again, and is eager to hear what I decide. I nod at him, but make no verbal commitment, and all the while, I continue to wait for a knock on the entrance door, letting me know that Kemina has come back. But I hear nothing. At nine I head upstairs to do homework on my bed, but I'm seriously distracted by the fact that she still hasn't returned. Finally, at about ten, Kemina knocks lightly on my doorframe.

"Hey, Justine." She sounds tentative. "Can I come in?"

I don't mean to sound all possessive and needy, but I kinda do. "It's late. Where have you been all this time?"

Kemina comes in and sort of floats over to my bed, and then sits on the edge. I sigh inside my heart, experiencing a messed-up sense of relief that she's near me again. She lifts her eyes to mine and inside them I see happiness. I'm suddenly sure things went well with Grant—and I just don't know what that means for her or for me. And yeah, I'm selfish as shit.

"I had dinner with Grant and then we went over to Nightingale and reviewed some files he had saved on his computer." Her gaze is steady on my face.

I feel jealous of Grant and, simultaneously, I feel guilty that I'm jealous. "What kind of files?"

"Ideas he has for a new line. You know how 'vixen' are really female foxes?"

I nod, never having given that too much thought. I always thought of vixen as hot and mischievous girls in sexy lingerie.

"Well, his idea is to develop a lingerie line called Real Foxes. As he explained it to me, he wants to expand the Nightingale Lingerie line to real-sized women."

Now she's searching my face for a reaction, but I wear a deliberate blank mask. And worse, I'm sarcastic. *"Real-sized?* Like you—six feet tall and a size four?"

Her face twists with hurt feelings—it's really quick and I almost miss it—but she responds to me with honesty, rather than more sarcasm. "I thought you'd be happy for me."

That's when the emotional dam inside me breaks and I spill. "Oh, Kemi, of course I'm happy for you!" And I am. I lean forward and hug her tightly. "This means you still have your job!"

"They were planning to go out and find a new plus-sized model, but instead they're going to go with, 'Baby Vixen, as in, me, grows up to be a Real Fox'. Grant wants to sign me to an exclusive. So I'll only be working for Nightingale. They want to do loungewear and some casual apparel, as well."

Despite how badly I wish it wasn't so, my insecurity is somehow still front and center in my mind. Part of me wishes she'd give up modeling altogether and just be another regular college kid. Like I'll be next year. But I manage to force the worry out of my voice cuz I know it isn't fair. "That sounds awesome, Kemi. Like a really good opportunity."

Kemina settles her long body beside me and leans back on the headboard. Her slender hand finds my thigh and I get goose bumps. "I'm at the right age—still a teenager, but also an adult—so my message will reach both teenage girls and adult women. Grant said I'll be the spokesperson."

"Your message? What will it be?"

She turns toward me and grabs my face in both of her hands. And she grins. Yup, she shoots me the crooked, ear-to-ear smile that I love. "My message is that it's fine to be *the real you. The real you*, in fact, is *perfect* just because it *is* you." She seems more confident with this plan than last time we talked. She doesn't even blush.

And when Kemi leans forward and kisses me, I start to relax. But the kiss is over too soon cuz her new message is still front and center in her mind. "Being beautiful has always been my life's purpose—I know how shallow it seems—and I had to struggle so hard to stay camera-perfect thin. Now, I'm really starting to believe I already *am* perfect. No more starving or over exercising. Just eating right and taking care of my body. This is my message, and I'll be in a position to show people that you can be beautiful and sexy while still being real!" She's so pumped she's almost shouting. "Plus, I told Grant I wanted to start my degree in Women's Studies at City College. He's totally supportive of the idea."

I hug her and she leans against my shoulder. When I hear her happy sigh, it hits me that she's finally starting to live her dreams, which is way cool.

I feel good—it's gonna be okay for her and for us, as far as I can see. And she must sense the calmness between us, too, cuz we sit there, very still, on my bed for about fifteen minutes, each of us caught up in our own thoughts about what it means for Kemina to become a *real* woman. It's peaceful, and I even have a chance to start working through the reasons for all my insecurity. But then I hear a short gasp from beside me. I look at Kemi, and then I follow her gaze.

We look through the window and watch as Mrs. Lopez trudges over to Kemina's bed, not seeming to be aware that we're staring at her from across the alley. She climbs beneath Kemi's covers and turns so that her back is facing us. And her shoulders start shaking and shuddering.

I think Mrs. Lopez is crying.

21

It's messed-up, but neither one of us asks about the other's mother. Maybe there's too much pain tied up in those kinda questions and neither of us is the type to go there on purpose. Or maybe we're still in the honeymoon stage of our relationship and it's somehow too soon to delve into the nitty-gritty of what makes each of us tick. Whatever the case, Kemina and I are both master avoiders and we steer clear of the messy and uncomfortable topic of mothers. Kemina *does* mention, in an offhand sort of way, that she's received a bunch of ranting and maybe even threatening *emails* from Scary-Mama about loyalty and family and how Kemina better not think she can just walk away. She refuses to show the emails to me, though. Not much I can do about them other than worry.

So for right now, I'm just down with having a girlfriend, taking her places, and showing her a good time. And I'd be lying if I didn't admit that I liked showing her off a little too. Not cuz she's "Kemina", but cuz she's mine.

So maybe I think of her as *my girl*, which I realize is so sixties R&B. But it's what she is.

"So, you guys are all seniors in high school, and you all are from the same neighborhood, but go to different high schools?" She asks.

Bart and Joey can only nod. They are still spellbound to the point of being tongue-tied by my former "Baby Vixen". I sincerely hope that they get over it soon. This shit is getting tiresome.

"And you guys both play on your high school teams? Well, I know you do Joey as we just watched you play." She giggles, which is very un-Kemina-like. But I can tell she's a little nervous, and is being cautious, and maybe even leery. Again I'm reminded that she has had few reasons to trust people.

Kemina has caused quite a stir tonight at the Cooper Village High School varsity boys' basketball game. For a second or two in the first quarter, Joey actually stood there, smack dab in the middle of the court, gaping up at her, when Kemina's voice rang out, "Go Fresco—number thirty-four!" A bunch of other players stopped to gawk at her when we were waiting for Joey outside the locker rooms. When she smiled and said to them, "Great game, Tigers!" I don't think they even remembered that they lost. And even if people didn't recognize her as Kemina, the Green Vixen, they recognized that she was *somebody*. Nearly six feet tall, beautiful and regal, I guess, she can't keep it a secret that she's someone special. So there was a lot of staring and whispering directed at her from both girls and boys. And parents. And teachers. But since there were miraculously no paparazzi around, Kemi seemed relatively relaxed.

The four of us sit at our usual upstairs table at the Naldo Café, eating pizza and drinking soda, and I can't miss that Kemi puts down a three deep dish slices with no problem.

"So I hear you're stayin' at Justine's place?" Bart asks. "What's wrong with your place across the alley?" On the way over here from the game, we filled the guys in that we'd met by flashing signs across an alley.

Kemina looks over at me and I can tell she's trying to decide whether to level with my friends or not. She chooses option B, *or not*. "This is just a temporary situation. My mother's... away." *As in, emotionally unavailable,* I think. I find myself wondering if her mom has been this cold since Kemi was a little girl.

The guys both nod and then they shove more pizza into their faces, and I decide that this time it's Kemina who's "away", not her mother.

"So, you gonna take Kemina to the prom?" Joey asks me.

Jeez, these guys know no boundaries with their questions. We might as well have paparazzi stalking us.

Kemi is still looking at me from before, and she waits for my answer. I have no idea if her idea of a good time is a cheesy high school prom, where the paparazzi would likely have a field day about us going together, so I'm not sure what to say. "Prob'ly," I mutter under my breath, and Kemina frowns a bit and then looks away from me.

"Well, tonight's a school night and my ma's gonna be expecting me home, so I'm gonna take off. But, before I go, can I get a selfie with ya, Kemina?" Joey stands up and moves beside Kemi before she even has a chance to answer. He then pushes his round cheek right up against her face and says, "Smile like ya love me."

She complies and doesn't even roll her eyes when Bart pushes Joey aside and takes his own selfie with her. They clearly have not yet moved beyond star struck into the realm of friendship, but I'm fairly certain that, if Kemi has some patience, they'll make the transition.

After we eat, Kemi and I walk, hand in hand, back to my apartment. Still no paparazzi in sight, which is cool, although she's recognized by plenty of people who walk past us. The reaction is always the same. People glance at her as if she's anyone else on the street, do a double take when they recognize "Kemina", stare at her for a few seconds, realize she's holding hands with someone, and then stare at me for a few seconds. I can tell when they look at me that they're trying to figure out "what" I am. *Is that a girl or a guy?* What *I* am will tell them if Kemina is straight or a lesbian. I just stare straight ahead of me and let them think whatever they want. But that doesn't stop them from snapping pictures of us with their phones, which pop up here and there on social media.

When we get to my building, Kemina looks over at her brownstone and I wonder if she *wants* to catch a glimpse of her mother, or if she's hoping to escape her mother's sight.

"Have you heard from your mother yet?" I'm a little nervous to ask.

"No. Other than those emails, Mama hasn't called or texted me." She doesn't remove her gaze from the building.

"You okay with not talking to her?"

"I guess." Kemi grabs my hand. "Let's go inside."

We hang our coats on the wall pegs in the entryway and together walk down the hall into the living room. It's late, but Dad and Pam are still up.

"Hey, girls." My dad stands up to greet us. He gives us each a quick hug, and then says quietly into my ear, "We were hoping you'd come in soon. Pam and I have something we'd like to discuss with you."

I immediately think of my mother. I just know they want to talk about why I'm being so stubborn about not seeing her, and all I can think of for a reason is that I'm falling in love and I don't want anything to ruin this magical time for me.

So sue me.

"Sure, Dad." I look down at Pam and she isn't her perky self. In fact her nose is a bit red and her eyes are puffy, as if she's been crying. Oddly, I experience an inexplicable surge of anger at my dad and I stifle the urge to ask him, "What the hell did you do to her?"

Pitiful Pam. I don't like seeing her this way.

"I'm tired, Justine. I'm going up to my room. Say good night to me when you come upstairs." Kemi must have gotten the family-only-chat-time vibe.

"'Kay. I'll be up in a few."

Dad nods toward the chair in the corner, so I sit in it.

"S'up you guys?" I try to be funny. "Who died?"

Dad and Pam exchange glances, and for a heart-stopping minute I actually think someone *has* died—like maybe my mother. It'd be just like her to go and die right now and ruin everything good in my life. And I know I'm an asshole for even thinking this.

"Well, it would be easier just to show you." Dad goes over to where Pam is sitting and he bends over to pick up a small box from the coffee table. A small black velvet box. He steps over to me and opens it. I already know what's inside before he pops it open. But there it is, staring me in the face—a beautiful, sparkling, and pretty freaking big, diamond ring.

"So why's Pam crying? Isn't it what she was after all along?" I sound like a bitch. I don't even know why I asked him those things. Pam, naturally, hears what I asked, and makes a rather failing attempt at stifling a sob.

I haven't seen Dad look so pissed-off at me in years. I can immediately tell how much he loves her and my heart melts a bit. "She won't say yes until you, as spokesperson for the kids, give us your blessing."

Time to step up to the plate. "Yeah, well, if you're asking me, I'm all for it."

Surprised, Pam looks up from her hands that are folded on her lap.

"You are?" Dad asks, his expression a cross between hopeful and relieved.

I'm still flippant. "Sure, why not?" Maybe they'll actually believe that this is no big deal to me.

But Dad is staring at me with round dark eyes, and I know I need to do better. For him. For my brothers. For Pam. And maybe even for me.

So I get up, cross the room, and kneel down right in front of Pam. And I look up into her clouded, but still pretty, light blue eyes. "I think you're great Pam. Great for this family." That's a start. I stop talking and wait, hoping someone else will contribute, but they don't, so I go on. "At first, Pam, it was like you weren't into the boys. And I wasn't cool with that. But I told you how it had to be in this family—how the boys had to come first—and you listened. And you actually changed. *Nobody* changes their ways, Pam—but you did."

With a smile, Dad sits back down and places an arm around his fiancée. Because we all know that's what she is—the lady Dad is gonna marry. Pam rubs her reddened nose and says in a voice so tiny and meek that I want to hug her, "I do so love your father, doll, but I want to do what is right for this family… and if you don't want another woman living in this house *permanently*, then I will refuse your father's offer."

An image of Jake, Jory, and Dad—three bachelors living in this apartment by themselves when I leave for college next year—flashes before my eyes. It feels very empty. Come to think of it, wasn't I actually considering commuting to college from home to avoid that very situation? And then I add to the image in my head, Pam's consistently positive and newly playful presence. And I know it's right. It's for the best.

"No worries, Pam. You belong with us." And then I make the ultimate un-Justine-like gesture and I reach up and hug her. "Congrats, you guys."

Time to make my graceful exit, I decide, and I get up and head to the stairs. "Gonna go say good night to Kemi."

They don't notice when I leave. They're busy celebrating.

"Knock, knock," I say and push the office door open. Kemi is in her bed wearing a cotton nightie that is definitely not Vixen lingerie, her face scrubbed clean of makeup, and she looks very young. "Hey, there. You ready to go to sleep?"

"Not until I say good night to you." I approach the bed. She pats the spot beside her. "Can you lie down with me for a while?"

I'm glad I closed the door behind me. "Uh...yeah." She snuggles in so she's lying flat beneath the blankets, and I drop down on top of the covers beside her. "You look real pretty tonight, Kemi."

"Right now? Without makeup and nice clothes?" Her voice is soft and dreamy.

"Yeah. Right now."

She turns on her side and puts her head on my shoulder. "What was going on downstairs? You know, when we got home?"

I clear my throat. "Nothing bad. Dad sort of proposed to Pam earlier in the night."

"Then why on earth was she crying?"

"She wouldn't say yes 'til she talked to me." I feel a rush of tears come to my eyes that I can't explain. I blink a whole bunch of times to fight them off. Crying is not my style. "She wanted my okay."

"You gave it?"

"Sure, she fits in great with our family. The boys need her... and Dad does, too."

"What about you, Justine?"

"I'm cool with it. I'm cool with her. I…uh…I think she loves us, you know?"

My girl allows me to be quiet for a while as the prospect of this new addition to my family sinks into my head. Finally, Kemina says something unexpected. "Mama was never what could be called a loving mother."

I want to see her face, however, at the moment it's tucked right under my chin. "But we saw her crying. She was lying in your bed last night and she was crying."

After a deep sigh, Kemina says, "That doesn't mean she loves me, Justine. I've lived with her for eighteen years. I've tried to get her to show her love for as long as I can remember. She would never do it."

I think about what Kemi just told me. It's nothing like how things were with Mom before she left. Sure, Mom was flighty and unreliable, but she was never cold.

"And all I could ever hear was her voice in my head telling me that I wasn't thin enough or smart enough or nice enough or good enough."

Neither one of us have ever opened up like this before and I don't want her to stop telling me her story. So I stay quiet.

"I never could understand why a girl would want to be my friend—not once in my whole life. I always wondered if a girl who said she was my friend had ulterior motives, because I believed my mother—nobody would *choose* to hang around me. Up until you."

"But I want to be more than just your friend." I wonder if that invalidates my importance in her life somehow.

"I know that, Justine… and truth be told, I've never been very trusting in the romantic area either."

I reach my arm around her and squeeze her shoulder.

"Mama's coldness has affected me in so many ways. But the biggest way is that I've never been able to see myself for how and who I really am. I think I'm starting to now, but…."

"But? But what?"

"But it doesn't mean I still don't crave her love. I just know I'm never going to get what it is I need from her. People don't change." As Kemi reaches up and rubs her eyes like she's pushing some stray tears back inside, I can't help but think of how much Pam changed. "All I get from Mama now are cruel emails and threatening notifications from her lawyer. It's not like I fired her. She's still my business manager. I don't get why she's so angry."

Kemina sounds sad and dejected. I want to say it isn't true, that her mom will change and become loving and supportive and warm, but I'd be lying. Like I said to Pam a little while ago, people almost never change, and I still believe that. "But at least you know now that it isn't your fault. It's nothing you did."

I hear a soft chuckle that I know isn't real laughter. "I'm starting to understand, Justine. It doesn't mean that it doesn't hurt, though. The fact that all I've heard from her are evils taunts and...." And that's when Kemi starts to cry. All I can do is hold her for the next few minutes.

"Kiss me, Justine." It is the first thing she says when she calms down enough to speak. Her words are breathless and needy, and without a thought I comply.

I lean over on top of her and seal my lips onto hers, swallowing the last of her sobs. I want so much to comfort her and for some reason, I want her to comfort me. This can only be done by touching each other—of that I'm certain. So I reach my hand inside the top of her nightgown and I curl my palm around the softness of her breast, which is heaving from the deep breaths she's taking to calm herself. She moans when my fingertips start to move and I moan because the power of this moment is comparable to nothing I've yet experienced in my life. I squeeze my thighs together, because it relieves the pressure of my urges, and I lift my lips from hers and slide them down over her jaw into the hollow of her neck.

Because of our position, I can only caress one of her breasts and only kiss one side of her neck. And Kemina seems so overwhelmed by physical sensation that she doesn't try to reciprocate, but instead just grasps my arms very tightly. I admit to myself this is how I want it at right now in my life. I'm not ready for full sexual intimacy, and Kemi has indicated that she's on the same page as far as that goes. Just touching Kemi is enough—it's life-changing in the way of sealing the truth of the fact that I'm a woman who wants to be with women. When I finally lean up on my side to look at my girlfriend, all I can think about is that I hope to see pleasure on her face. And I do. Beyond this moment being enough, it's also completely perfect.

After a minute or two, she takes a deep breath and says very quietly, "I counted up all the injuries in my heart, Justine—wounds from Mama's emotional distance and cruel words that have been building up since I was a little girl. There are just so many. But now it's time for me to start getting over this. And I'm ready for the fact that I have to be alone, without her, to heal."

I know one thing for sure, and I tell her. "You aren't alone." She's done some major thinking, has already suffered some serious pain, and is trying to leave the past behind to move on to a brighter present. I'll be right there beside her.

For just a second I wonder when I'll come to terms with the screwed-up situation involving my own mother, but like always I push it out of my mind.

Getting up off the bed, I lean down to give my girl one more kiss. As I walk to the door, I hear her say softly, "I've never been to a prom. Always wanted to go to one."

Kemina just keeps giving me more reasons to smile.

22

Life happens. No matter what pain and anguish you're going through, the world doesn't stop turning so that you can get off and take a little break, and then stop again so you can hop back on when you've got your ducks in a row. So we keep on doing our own things as well as things together, and Kemina doesn't offer too much in the way of information about what's going on with her mother. But I've never walked in on her in the middle of a heart-to-heart phone conversation with her mom, and I've noticed that Mrs. Lopez no longer sleeps in Kemi's bed. So, it seems that where there was once coldness between them, now there's ice. And life goes on.

Kemina keeps very busy with her Real Foxes campaign for Nightingale, which she is developing with Grant Pederson. He's told her that she's actually a bit too thin for what he has in mind, so she's on something of a reverse diet. I personally think Kemi looks great with the extra curves. And for her body type, I don't really think they are extra. I think the pounds were meant to be there and she starved herself to fight them off. I've always been kind of naturally lean and lanky, and I'm cool with myself this way, but I like to see Kemi looking healthy, and not being hungry.

Preseason softball has started up, and I'm this year's captain. In the past, I always lived for softball, but I have so much more going on in my life this year that I see it as a commitment not just as a sport I love. Today Dad meets me at the end of softball practice and Coach Jenkins lets me take an extra batting practice so he can watch. After I shower, Dad tells me that Pam is feeding the boys and that he's gonna take me out to dinner. We end up at a corner Italian place, one of those quaint little restaurants that serve real Italian food with old world charm, and I immediately know he wants to talk about something specific. I lose my appetite.

After we order, I just come right out and ask him. "So why'd you bring me here, Dad?" I sip my water, brush my fingers through my short hair, and then look at him squarely. "Pam already asked me if I'd be her maid of honor, and I already said yes, as long as I don't have to wear a dress, or tell anyone I am a maid of anything."

Dad smiles in that patient way he has mastered through years of solo parenting. "I think that's awesome, Jussy, and I know that Pam is very pleased. It's going to be only family and a few close friends, so don't worry, we won't broadcast the whole *maid* of honor thing."

"Cool. The wedding's on for this summer, right?"

"Yes, we'll be man and wife before you leave for Marymount Manhattan. And you can rest assured that the boys will be well-fed and cared for, and loved, of course. So, no worries."

"You notice that Jory isn't as emo lately and Jake isn't as jazzed?" This fact has been on my mind for a while. I'm pretty sure it's a good thing.

Dad nods and butters a roll. "I think it is a result of them feeling secure. Pam has been great with them."

"But all this Pam talk is not why you brought me here, is it?"

"Can't a guy take his daughter out for Italian without being second-guessed?"

"Um...no. So spill it, Dad."

He has the good grace to look guilty. "You got me. So I'll just put it out there. It's about your mother."

I'm not even slightly surprised. "What about her?"

"She wants to see you and the boys."

"And?"

"And I think you should see her."

The waiter comes at this strategic moment, and serves me my ravioli that I'm frankly not in the mood for and Dad some kind of an Italian fish dish that actually repulses me a little bit. After he refills our waters and asks us a few waiter-questions, he leaves and I practically shout, "Why?"

"Why what?"

I want to shake him. "Why do you think I should see her? I mean, *you* really should be more pissed-off at her than I am! She left you with three kids to raise so she could go party!"

"You know it isn't exactly that simple, Justine."

"What part of it?"

"The part where she had a full choice in what she did—in leaving us. Honey, she's an addict. She was very likely an alcoholic way back when I first met her, and she stopped drinking for a while, but when you guys were kids she reverted to her old ways."

"And then some," I add, thinking of the drugs.

"Your mother didn't leave us intentionally. And you know what I'm saying is true."

I want to stop talking about this for a while so I force myself to eat even though I'm not particularly hungry. Dad takes the hint, and he does the same.

When we're finished, I ask the question I need the answer to, one more time. "Why are you doing this for her? You're getting married. If I were you, I'd just let Mom fall completely out of the picture."

Dad shakes his head and I'm curious about what he's thinking cuz he's actually a pretty smart guy. "Jussy, I'm not going to bat for *your mother*. I'm going to bat for *you.*"

For me?

I must be looking at him like he's nuts cuz Dad actually reaches across the table and takes my hand in his. "She's your mother. And no, it's not a pretty situation. It isn't how any of us, including her, would have planned it. But she's still your mother and I don't want you to have to live with any regrets."

Regrets? Mom is the one who has reason to have regrets. Why would I be saddled with regrets over what *she* did to *us*? "*Hello!* I didn't create this problem, Dad!"

"But you're almost eighteen years old now, and you're responsible for your choices. *And* you have to live with them— not just this year and next. Forever, Justine." Dad places his napkin on the table. "Just give it some thought, that's all I ask. I promise if you think it over, I'll stop nagging you about it."

I nod in reluctant agreement and then excuse myself to go to the restroom while Dad pays. And when I look in the mirror in the bathroom, I see someone who really doesn't have a clue what to do next looking back at me.

23

Kemi has been out late for the past few nights. She and Grant have been meeting with some very upscale fashion designers. I miss her a lot but she's pretty excited, so I'm trying to be excited for her. I admittedly must fight a level of insecurity cuz she's living a glamorous life and I'm living the life of a regular high school senior. But I've decided to go easy on myself cuz my feelings are normal.

Recently, she's had to go out and buy some new clothes for some of these meetings because it's important for her to look professional. Most of her clothes and shoes are still in her bedroom in her old apartment, and she hasn't yet been back over there to get them. So, when she isn't home tonight by ten, I'm not particularly worried cuz I think maybe she went clothes shopping again. At eleven, I call her and it goes straight to voicemail, which makes me wonder. She usually picks up when I call. But when she's still not home at midnight, I'm definitely concerned.

Finally, I go upstairs to my bedroom, thinking that I'll go to sleep and when I wake up in the morning Kemina will be in her bed, but when I glance across the alley into her old bedroom, a few things catch my attention. First of all, the floor lamp in the corner of her bedroom is turned on. There have been no lights on in her room since the last time her mother slept in there, so I find this odd. And second, there are two big suitcases on the bed, both packed almost full of clothes, but still lying open, as if Kemina was interrupted while she was packing. I don't see Kemi or her mother.

Suddenly, I get a really cold, scared feeling in my heart, and I decide not to ignore it. My instinct tells me to interpret the open suitcases as a sign. Kemi was in that bedroom earlier tonight, packing her clothes and, in a way, saying good-bye to her old way of life—when something stopped her. Or more likely, *someone* stopped her.

I ask myself exactly how angry Kemina's mother is at her. I know I can only find the answer by checking the emails on her laptop. So, again feeling like a voyeur, but knowing I'm doing this for her benefit, I go downstairs and into the office, find Kemi's laptop, place it on the desk, and check her emails.

Subject: Daughter of Mine.

I will not take this insult lying down. If you think you can just walk away without looking back, you are dead wrong. I made you into what you are. Face it, young lady, without my hard work you would be nothing but a fat, stupid whale. You owe me.

Subject: Kemina.

You expect me to be appreciative that you didn't fire me as your business manager? Thankful that I still have a salary? It doesn't work that way, Kemina. I thought you were smart enough to know that. You can't walk away from me. If you think you and that dyke across the alley are going to stroll away together for a happily ever after under a rainbow flag, you'd better think again. It is not going to happen.

Subject: A fucking plus-size model?

That'll be the day. You'll be the laughingstock of professional models. I need to make my move before your ass gets any wider than it already is. You'll thank me for it when you get down off of the lipstick lesbian cloud you are currently floating on—of that

I'm certain. Come back to your house and your mother and the
right way to live.

And there are more of the same. But I don't have time right
now to read them all. Instead, I carry her laptop to my father's
bedroom and knock on the door.

"Jory? Jake?" Surprisingly, it's Pam's voice I hear. "You
boys okay?"

"Uh… no, it's me."

Pam comes to the bedroom door, wrapping herself in a silky
aqua robe that seems to match the silky aqua negligee beneath it.
Definitely Vixen Lingerie, I find myself thinking. "Doll, what's
wrong?"

"Can I come in? I want to show Dad… or, *you guys,*
something."

"Of course." I look past her into the bedroom. Dad is
yawning and pushing himself up to a sitting position. Within
thirty seconds, I have the laptop open on their bed and I'm filling
them in on how Kemi didn't return home, and about the suitcases
on the bed in her old room across the alley.

"So you think her mother has *kidnapped* her?" Dad asks me,
and the question sort of puts this whole thing into perspective. I

wonder if I'm overreacting, but somehow my gut tells me I'm not.

"Maybe more like detained her, against her will," I reply feebly.

"Are you suggesting we should call the police?" He's trying to get a clear picture of what I want.

I think about it for a minute. "Maybe we should just go over there."

"You think her mother is actually going to let us in if we buzz?" Dad is looking at me strangely now and I realize that I don't have a clue what he's thinking. "Maybe we should wait until the morning. You know, to see if she comes back overnight. And if she doesn't we can go over there and ask Mrs. Lopez if she's seen Kemina."

"No." Pam steps into the conversation. "We need to go over there right now. Justine *knows* Kemina. If she didn't return home, answer calls or texts, and appears to have been interrupted while she was packing, and Justine thinks something is wrong, then we need to listen to her."

A flood of warmth for this woman who is soon to be my stepmother rushes in on me. I'm speechless. Dad gets up off his bed and heads to the wingback chair in the corner where his clothes from yesterday have been tossed. He pulls jeans on over his boxers. "Who am I to argue with two smart ladies?" He asks as he puts on his Black Dog sweatshirt. "You two stay here. I'll go see what's up."

Pam nods but I just follow him down the hall and out the door.

We don't even get to the bottom of our outdoor steps when the picture of what's going on becomes crystal clear. Mrs. Lopez's BMW is double-parked and running in front of the building, with the trunk open and no one in the driver's seat. Somebody is sitting alone in the backseat. It's too dark outside to tell who it is, but I'm pretty sure I already know. I run over to the car.

"Justine, wait for me!" Dad shouts, but I don't listen.

I press my face to the glass of the backseat window and I can see that it's Kemi inside. She has a long piece of ripped cloth tied around her face, and something is stuffed inside her mouth as well. The car door isn't locked, so I open it and pull Kemi out. I can't miss that her wrists are zip-tied behind her back. I stop and stare and have a complete "what the hell?" moment. Kemi stares back. I don't know whose shock is greater.

Dad comes to his senses well before we do. As soon as he reaches us, he yanks the cloth that is tied around her mouth down underneath her chin and pulls what appears to be a washcloth out of her mouth.

Kemi sucks in a huge breath and then falls against my father, in a sort of half faint, but she soon finds enough composure to say, "She's coming right back—we've gotta get out of here! She's just inside getting her suitcase and she'll be right back!" I've never seen Kemi quite this frantic—so very different from the confident girl I've seen lately. Her face is tear-stained, her whole body is trembling, and she has to hold onto my father and me, or I'm pretty sure she'd fall. She's a mess. And I feel like she looks.

Just then Pam trots down the stairs in her light pink sweat suit, and she announces, "I've already called 9-1-1. Now, Justine, help Kemina over here and we can sit on the steps until the police show up." She walks toward us and helps me to support Kemina, whose arms are still tied behind her back.

"No! Not the police—Mama'll be so mad! Let me just go inside and call back the police and tell them it was a false alarm."

Just then Mrs. Lopez scrambles down the steps of her building. "Let go of my daughter! She is coming with me!" She tries to run over to me and Pam and Kemi, but my dad kind of scoops her into his arms and restrains her. "Let me go! Leave me alone! Stay out of our family business!"

Kemi's mother is basically ranting and raving. In my opinion, her behavior has "restraining order" written all over it. I can tell Dad doesn't want to be too rough, but the woman is kicking and clawing at him. He refuses to let go, and thankfully the police show up in a matter of a couple minutes.

This whole scene is surreal—I can't believe it's happening. And it doesn't take long until there are neighbors, woken up by the noise and the lights, and soon photographers, dotting the sidewalk. The police arrest Kemi's mom, which is unfortunately very well documented by photographers, and then they block off the street. Thankfully, after the cops free Kemi's wrists from the zip ties, they let us escort her into our living room to answer questions there.

Kemi refuses to go in an ambulance to the hospital. Other than cuts to her wrist from the tight plastic ties, which she lets Pam clean and bandage, and the three whitish lines on her face that are left over from being scratched last week, she's physically unharmed. I suspect that her mental health is a far different story. When the police finally leave, Dad and Pam let me to go with Kemi up to the office.

But before I leave the room, I ask Dad and Pam, both. "Can I stay in the room with Kemi for the rest of the night? I think she needs me."

And again, Pam steps forward. "Of course you can stay with her tonight, doll. Go take care of your girl."

I smile at Pam because she gets me. Kemi and I more or less stagger up the stairs.

Fifteen minutes later we are snuggled together in the guest room bed, which has become "Kemi's bed", in my mind.

Her voice is still shaky when she says, "You saved my butt again, Justine."

"I just kinda knew something was off. It's like, I just had this feeling you were in trouble." I then tell her about the suitcases and confess about checking out the emails on her laptop.

"You did what you had to do so you could help me. Who knows where Mama would have taken me if you hadn't come outside?" Kemi finally allows a sob. "And she's... she's my mother!"

I can hear the disbelief in her voice. Disbelief that the person who is supposed to love and cherish and care for her the most could turn on her like this. I know it's devastating, mostly because it was so intentional—calculated even. An evil characteristic my own mother doesn't share.

And that's when I decide. I'm gonna meet with my mother. Somewhere inside, I know that what Mom did to our family wasn't in any way designed to hurt us or show us or teach us. Mom was just battling her own demons and her family got caught in the crossfire.

Kemina cries for longer than I expect, and I know she needs to get it out, so I don't try to stop her. Instead, I think about how I can meet up with Mom, and not get my heart broken in the process. Cuz even if Mom doesn't hurt me on purpose, her actions still cause lots of pain. I decide that the best way to protect myself is by putting boundaries on the relationship until I know she can be trusted. I can get to know Mom gradually. And we're gonna need to talk about why we lost her to booze and drugs in the first place, so I understand it. Plus she's gonna have to somehow convince me it's not gonna happen again.

But at this moment I accept that her absence from my life was not a cold and calculated effort to hurt me. Probably cuz I've had a front row seat to watch a mother cause intentional pain in her daughter's life and I recognize the difference in my own circumstances. But I don't mention this recognition to Kemi. It'd only hurt her more. Make her feel more alone, as if she's the only unloved daughter on the planet.

"It's going to be so hard to work through this." Her voice is ragged from the crying. "All of the legalities and then criminal charges and the publicity and...." She allows her voice to trail away but she doesn't start crying again.

"Tonight's probably not the best night to think about it." I pull her into my arms and run my fingers lightly over the mostly-healed scratch marks on her face. "We'll deal with all of it. I've got faith in your strength, I saw it with my own eyes as you moved forward in your life with Real Foxes, even though you were hurting."

"That feels like a million years ago."

I stick my thumb and index finger on the back of her neck and try to rub away her stress. "It was only just this morning that you were taking on the world. We'll get you back there, no worries." I feel strong and capable, in a way that's all new to me. "Sometimes you've just gotta let these things unfold on their own. No good will come from worrying. Let's just... let's just think about the prom instead."

"The prom?"

"Yes. Kemina. I've been meaning to ask you, wanna be my date to the UWSAA senior prom?"

She laughs and it sounds so good. "Of course, if you want."

"Oh, I want," I tease.

"Are you going to wear a tuxedo?"

"You better believe it. Now let's talk colors for your dress." I figure Kemi might enjoy a fashion discussion even if I'm completely inept.

"Maybe I want to wear a tuxedo, too," Kemina says, catching me off guard.

We talk about the prom until Kemina falls asleep in my arms.

24

I want the meeting with my mother to take place somewhere I'm comfortable, but not at home. Not ready for that yet. So I asked Dad to tell her to meet me at Naldo's Café today after softball practice. I sit here holding a cup of hot cocoa against my chest, staring at the cup that's waiting for my mother on the table across from me. I wonder if she still likes hot cocoa. She used to love it when I was a kid. It was her absolute favorite—she'd take cocoa over coffee or tea any day. Then I wonder if she's even gonna show up. Mom's been a no-show for more than a few mother-daughter meetings over the past five years.

But I see her coming down the street through the café's glass wall, and I'm not sure whether to be relieved or disappointed. The way Mom moves is different from the last time I saw her on the sidewalk in front of my building. She's not shuffling along like every step is an effort, as much as she's just walking like anybody else on the street. Her eyes meet mine as soon as she sees where I'm sitting and she doesn't look away, even as she pushes the glass door open and steps through.

I stand up when she gets to the table, kinda like a real gentlemen would, and I hope like hell she won't try to hug me. Thankfully, she doesn't.

Time for Justine Laraby's stupid comment. "Got you a cup of hot cocoa. Hope you still like it."

Mom smiles, and it's a sad, gentle smile. I notice she's had her tooth fixed. I figure Dad must have helped her with that. From what I hear, homeless people don't have great dental benefits. "I love hot cocoa, Justy. Thank you."

Justy. She called me Justy.

It's pretty busy where I'm sitting. People push past and one lady even bumps my head with her shoulder bag. I didn't choose the usual private table for Kemi and me, up in the loft. I went for a downstairs table where most of the other customers are hanging out. Safety in numbers had been my table-choosing philosophy.

I study my mother silently for a long minute—how her hands don't fumble or shake when she removes the plastic cover from the cup, how her brown eyes look clear and bright, how her clothes, though wrinkled, look clean and don't smell like cigarettes and pee—and a flicker of hope that things can be different kindles in my heart.

I stomp on it. Over and over again, I stomp on it 'til it's gone.

"So your father's getting married this summer?"

"Yeah." I don't offer her my feelings about Perfect Pam, my stepmother-to-be. I just don't.

"Are you happy about it?"

"Very."

Mom nods and takes a sip of her drink. She manages to avoid getting one of those tiny and adorable cocoa mustaches that Pam always ends up with, and Dad wipes away with love in his eyes. "How's your softball season going?"

I don't know why, but the question causes a stab of pain to my heart. Like I know that if she was a real mother, she'd know how softball was going, and she wouldn't have to ask. But still I answer briefly. "It's good. I've scored at least one run at every game." Like this actually matters in the bigger scheme of things.

"That sounds like the Justy I know."

Knew. I think so loud that she can probably hear. *The Justy you knew.*

"H-how... how are the boys?" Her eyes are suddenly shadowed, and I can tell this is a hard question for her to ask.

I shrug. "Pretty good, I guess." And suddenly I don't give a crap if I hurt her. "They're nuts about Pam, the lady Dad's gonna marry."

Mom nods, and then she smiles that sad smile again. "Good. I'm happy to hear that."

I sincerely wish the time to cut through the polite bullshit had already arrived, but apparently it isn't here yet. We exchange a few more pleasantries about the freaking weather, and then Mom fills me in about the halfway house where she's living right now, and how she's trying to get a job stocking shelves at some grocery store in Queens. I do my smiling, nodding best and I fight against the urge to peek at the clock on the wall.

How much longer do I have to stay to make this visit official?

Then she makes her move. "Justy, I know you've heard this song and dance from me before, and I know that only time will tell, but I'm clean now. It's been a while, too—my longest stretch of sobriety in the past five years."

I bite back the remark I want to make, which goes something like this: "So I suppose it's gonna be *different* this time?"

She continues speaking. "I know what I've done to your life—your lives—and I'm sorry. I need you to know that. But I'm not going to beat myself up any further because when I do that I end up right back in the same black hole. Just understand that I'm sorry for making the choices I made, and I'm trying to make things right now."

"Don't you think it might be a little too late?" My voice trembles.

Again a dark cloud passes by her face, and she replies, "I sure hope not."

We're both quiet for a while, until I ask the question that's been burning in my mind. "What do you want from me, Mom?"

She sighs, and it's loud enough to remind me of Kemina's noisy sighs that night we met on the rooftop in the early spring. "Another chance, I guess."

"A chance to do what?"

Her first answer didn't "answer" anything. I need to know why she's really here.

Mom allows another sigh, and then offers another answer. "Look, I know I have no legs to stand on in the mothering department, so I was hoping that we could start out by just rebuilding a bond—by maybe being friends."

"I've got enough friends." It's curt, but it's also true.

"Maybe you should tell me what it is *you* want, Justine." I can tell that she desperately wants to look away from my angry eyes, but she doesn't.

"What would you say if I told you I still want a mother? Maybe not a perfect mother—maybe just a freaking damaged, broken-but-trying-to-be-in-one-piece-again mother. But a *mother*. What would you say to that?"

When she smiles this time it isn't as sad. "I'd say that it sounds like a plan to me."

We nod at each other and I suck down the last drop of my cocoa. Then I offer an olive branch. "If you aren't busy, I have a home softball game after school on Friday. You can come, if you want." Here's where it could get sticky, but if she can't handle the truth it's best I find out early. "My girlfriend is gonna be there. You can meet her."

Mom doesn't even blink. "I'll be there. And I'll look forward to saying hello to your girlfriend."

If it had been a test, she'd have passed. I stand up. "Okay, them. I'm gonna head out. I'll see you on Friday."

I don't try to hug her and she doesn't grab my sleeve and pull me against her. I guess we both figure there's plenty of time for that stuff in the future.

"Later." I turn and leave the café, and I feel a new hopefulness that I have to wonder about.

25

It feels like my first time ever at the plate. Like I'm some kind of a virgin hitter. First time at bat, I swing at anything and everything and I strike out. My teammates stare at me in shock and horror as I walk back to the dugout with my head down. I've never been so easily dealt with by a pitcher. And if possible, the second time at bat I'm even worse. I never swing at all. As I do my walk of shame back to the dugout this time, I strain to find where Kemina is sitting in the stands. And she's there, in her usual spot on the right side, about halfway up, as is my mother, who I'm trying very hard *not* to see. I can't miss her, though, cuz she's sitting maybe three rows behind Kemi.

I stare at my mom. Part of me is in complete disbelief that she actually came here today. That she did what she said she was gonna do. The other part of me wishes she would fall off the bleachers, anything to make her stop gawking at me. But she doesn't fall; she just waves. It's a kinda tentative hope-it's-okay-that-I'm-here sort of wave that I don't return. Instead, I look to Kemi, who doesn't make a gesture of any sort, but just smiles. And then she winks, which is unusual for her and it makes me think. I contemplate how awesome my girlfriend is and how lucky I am to have her, and then my mind wanders a little bit to other stuff that has to do with kissing her.

Turns out, that little smile and wink was just what I needed to get my head in the game. I know that sounds wrong, cuz being all horny should be something that takes my mind *out* of the game. But in this case it makes me forget that my mom is watching me play baseball for the first time in way too many years. Instead, I concentrate on how much I want Kemi, and when it comes time for my third at bat, I hit one out of the park.

After the game, my small crowd of devoted fans, Kemi, Dad, the twins, Pam, and Mom, meet me behind the dugout. It's a messed-up scene. The boys stand behind Dad and Pam, chowing down on foot long hot dogs from the Snack Shak, not even making an attempt to talk to Mom. They don't say so much as a hello. Kemi stands beside Pam and keeps smiling at me in this I-got-your-back way that I appreciate. And Mom leans on the building, stiff and rigid and really uncomfortable-looking, and all

I can think is that she's gonna bolt from the baseball diamond and go get high, cuz it's clear that this moment in time is sucking for her. I know it sucks for me.

But she surprises me by taking in a deep breath and standing up a bit taller, and then saying, "That was quite a hit you had in the fifth inning, Justy."

Dad steps in, eager to smooth out the situation so we can all breathe easier. "I'll wager it landed somewhere in Times Square, what do you think?"

"Oh, yes! I thought the very same thing!" Pam agrees eagerly and I can see that she's trying to whisk the boys out in front of her, so they'll say hi to Mom. But they aren't having any part of that.

"Mom, you know Pam, right?" I ask.

"Yes, we met one evening over dinner," Mom replies. I have no clue when that took place, but I figure the three of them must have had one hell of a long discussion about their goals for the boys and me and our relationship with Mom, cuz they're presenting a totally united front here.

"Well, I'd like you to meet my girlfriend, Kemina Lopez." Mom either has a good poker face or she's been too drunk and stoned for the past year to be aware that Kemi is a famous underwear model. She doesn't do the "OMFG—I know who you are!" thing with her eyes, but then, Mom always had a laid-back attitude, if I remember correctly.

She reaches out and shakes Kemi's hand and simply says, "It's nice to meet you, Kemina."

Kemi just nods. She isn't too trusting in mothers as a whole, and for good reason.

We all stand there awkwardly, and I worry that Dad is gonna force the boys to interact with Mom, but he's clued in and he doesn't. Instead, he says, "We're all going to go get smoothies at the deli on the corner, Laura. Would you car to join us?"

But Mom slowly shakes her head. "No, sorry, I can't. I have to get to work."

After another majorly awkward silence, I say, "Well, thanks for showing up here." Then I blush cuz that was probably the stupidest thing I've ever said.

"I didn't want to miss it, Justy. When is your next home game?" Her scared brown eyes are looking right into mine. She's taking a risk. "Maybe I could come to see it."

I nod. "Sure. Um, I'll get your number from Dad and I'll text you the day and time."

"Thank you, Justine." She then takes a step over toward the boys. Jory and Jake keep their gazes fastened on their sneakers. "And maybe I can take you guys out for ice cream next time."

The boys don't even shrug to indicate they heard her. They, like Pam and Dad, are presenting a united front. It's a united front that makes me think of a stone wall, but I can't blame them. They barely know our mother.

"That sounds great, Laura." Pam saves the day. I'm growing more and more fond of her every minute. "The boys never refuse a chance to eat ice cream."

Mom tries to smile, though I can tell it costs her, cuz Pam, however kind she may be, knows her sons better than she does. My mother then offers a quiet goodbye. I decide our first "play date" with Mom went about as well as could be expected.

I don't think forgiveness happens instantly—in my humble opinion it's more of a gradual process. In any case, after the next softball game, Dad and Pam excuse themselves, saying they have to be at some upscale bakery in less than thirty minutes to sample wedding cakes. I know that they're offering Mom a chance to have some alone time with the boys and me. Kemina is at a business meeting so she's not here to distract us from the pain of this evening, either.

At first, the boys balk about being mostly alone with Mom, to the tune of Jory pretty much shouting in a panicked voice, "Pam, Dad! You *gotta* come with us!" And then there's Jake, who licks his lips and says, "I wanna sample the wedding cakes. Sounds like too much fun to miss. I wanna go with you, Dad."

But Dad and Pam are adamant that they want their wedding cake to be a surprise to all of their guests, so they have to do this job alone. Grudgingly, the boys agree to have dinner and dessert with Mom and me, and since we're all familiar with Naldo's Café, that's what I suggest when my mom asks where we should eat.

When we get there, we order a pizza and some side dishes of pasta and meatballs and then we sit in total silence as we wait for the food to cook. After fifteen agonizing minutes of quiet, Mom and I go and pick up the food. Once we place it on the table and the boys dig in, it becomes a bit more relaxed between us.

I figure I'll be the one with the balls, so to speak, and I start the conversation. "Mom, Jory and Jake are both members of the art club at their middle school." Yeah, I know it's weak, but the twins really like art club and I hope maybe it will spark their interest in conversation.

She looks at me, then at them, and says, "I didn't know you guys were artists." *Not a good reply, Mom.*

"That's cuz you don't know nothin' about us." Jory is his usual blunt self. He forks a meatball and stuffs the entire thing into his mouth. His eyes bulge a bit as he chews.

Jake looks up at me and his eyes are as round as Jory's meatball. He waits to see what happens next.

Mom rises to the challenge. "I know, Jory. You're right. I have been absent for much of your childhood. And I'm very sorry about that."

Jory shovels another whole meatball into his mouth and as his eyes bulge, I worry I'm gonna have to give him the Heimlich maneuver. Jake just sits there staring at me.

"But I want to change that, boys. I want to start to be a part of your life."

I now understand the meaning of the expression, "the silence was deafening."

"I can't change the fact that I was gone. And I regret it so much, you'll never know. All I can do now is try to do better. To be a better person and a better mother to all three of you." Her eyes are wet as she looks from Jake to Jory, and then to me, and I wait for the first tear to drop. It doesn't take long until tears are streaming down her face. But I don't comfort her or try to get her to stop crying. Jake and Jory need to see her tears, as they have shed many of their own over her. "Please say you'll give me the chance."

Jake looks at Jory, and then at me. He simply shrugs and says, "Okay." And then he turns his attention to his half-eaten slice of pepperoni and bacon pizza.

Jory isn't as easy. "Not too sure I buy what yer sellin' here… uh…*Mom*."

Mom nods, and I know she gets it. "I'm going to try my best Jory. That is all I can do." She lets that sink into his head. "So… do you have any pictures of your art on your cell phones, boys? I would love to see what you've made."

Good move, Mom, I think. At this point, there's nothing left to be said in regard to her long absence.

Jake doesn't even finish chewing when he replies, "Justine has loads of pics."

I grab my phone and show Mom the finest works of Jake and Jory Laraby. She "ooohs and aaahs" over them, just enough without going overboard.

Jory can't resist commenting. "See that clay robot that's painted silver and red. It took me *three* art club meetings to make that one."

"Your hard work really shows, Jory. I would love to see some of these pieces in person," Mom keeps her eyes on the pictures on my phone.

"We have a lot of 'em in our bedroom," Jake informs her.

"Maybe…maybe like sometime you could come over and check 'em out." Jory's offer hangs in the air, and I think we all wait to see if he'll take it back. But he doesn't. He just adds, "You know, like sometime."

"Well, that sounds almost like a plan, Jory." Mom uses her napkin to dry her eyes. "Now, I heard that you guys like ice cream. What do you say we throw away our trash and get in line for ice cream cones?"

Jory and I nod, but Jake asks, "Is it cool if I get a sundae? I like hot fudge and strawberry sauce on chocolate ice cream with whipped cream and lots of nuts!"

"Of course it's okay. But it's better than okay if you let me have a taste!" Mom laughs. "What kind of ice cream sundae do you like, Jory?"

And the slow process of family forgiveness is underway.

26

Kemi and I sit together at the kitchen table, each working on our own projects. I'm writing an English essay, where the topic is to discuss a concept in life that has made you think deeply and inspired you to change, and I have chosen the concept of perfection. Kemina is pouring over pages upon pages of legal documents that will separate her business interests from her mother's. She looks kinda depressed, and I acknowledge that this isn't how she wanted things to turn out with her mom. There's a pending court case in regard to her mother's misdemeanor assault charge and all of the legal business bullshit, for her to deal with. But Mrs. Lopez actually made the process a little bit easier for Kemi by suing her and publicly ridiculing her "dyke daughter." Since her mother made those choices, Kemi's past sense of loyalty, obligation, and intimidation have pretty much faded, and have been replaced by a need for autonomy and a fair division of the "Kemina" assets.

"How does this sound, Kemi?" She looks up and nods, encouraging me to read what I wrote. "My life experiences over the past several months have given me reason to change my idea of what perfection really is. This Italian proverb expresses my need for a new philosophy very well: *He that will have a perfect brother must resign himself to remain brotherless.* In other words, nobody is perfect, and if you're holding off on having relationships, waiting for perfect people to come along, you're going to have a long and lonely wait. Perfection cannot be set in a certain shape that dries like concrete. Perfection, as I now understand it, is fluid. To be constantly improving. To be always trying to get better in ways that matter."

My girl blinks back tears, something she's been doing a lot lately. "That's amazing. I didn't know you could write like that."

I'm happy with the compliment, but I still want to cheer her up. So I bring up her favorite topic. "Anyway, have you and Grant set a date for that big runway show for the announcement of the Real Foxes line?"

She pushes away the legal documents so she can put her elbows on the table in front of her. And like I hoped, her eyes light up. "We're aiming for November. Like early November."

"Hopefully it doesn't turn out to be during either of our midterms," I say. Kemi's gonna take a couple of Women's Studies classes at City College in the fall.

"Hopefully not."

All of a sudden, Kemina grabs one of my notebooks and a pen, opens it up to a blank page, and scribbles something down in big letters. She flips the notebook to show me her message.

I couldn't have done all this without the support from you and your family.

I snatch up the notebook, turn to a fresh page, and write my response.

All this? Explain plz.

I slide the notebook back to her and she writes again.

Standing up to my mother. Separating from her even though it hurts. Being a real woman and liking it. Going to college.

I get up and walk around the table. The signs have served their purpose, and for them we have come to the window time and again, but now I want my next message to be delivered up close and personal. I reach out my hand to my girl, and she takes it and stands up in front of me.

"I really want a kiss. Starving for one, in fact," I admit, and I don't even blush.

Kemi smiles that poster-girl smile and then looks at me with honest, promise-filled eyes. "That can be arranged, Justine. *Nobody* goes hungry in this relationship."

Epilogue

I never knew a girl could look so hot in a tuxedo. But then, it's no ordinary tuxedo. And then there's the small detail that Kemi's no ordinary girl.

For tonight's prom, she borrowed a cream-colored woman's tuxedo from Grant, who offered to lend it to her from Nightingale wardrobe storage, as it was used several years back in a Vixen bra advertisement. In the ad, the model wore the tuxedo jacket wide open, the black cummerbund and a black lacey bra peeking out from beneath it. For the prom, Kemi feels it necessary to wear a white blouse underneath, and I totally agree with that decision, although she'd look stellar in just the bra. Her tuxedo pants are narrow and she rocks high black pumps that have her towering over me.

I wear a more traditional all-black tux, a classic white shirt, and a black bow tie. Before we enter the building, we strike a deal of sorts with the photographers who are stalking us. Kemi and I offer to give them an unrushed photo session out in front of the Empire State Restaurant and Lounge, where our prom is being held, and will even indulge them by answering a few questions, and in exchange we'll be free to enjoy the prom without paparazzi presence.

We did our part, and so far, it seems, they're sticking to the deal.

In defense of the media as a whole, they've been really cool about the "Nightingale Lingerie's Kemina comes out as a lesbian" thing. In fact, over the past few months, we've been photographed quite a few times in public together—holding hands and stuff—and social media has more or less embraced us as a couple. Maybe it's cuz we're a novelty and we give people yet another reason to tune in to entertainment shows or online gossip websites and buy their celebrity-filled magazines, or maybe it's cuz the world, as a whole, just doesn't give a shit anymore if a beautiful young model is straight or a lesbian. But the fear Mrs. Lopez once expressed about the public turning against a lesbian model has been what you could call unfounded.

Back at my apartment before we left for the prom, there was no paparazzi presence. Dad, Pam, and Mom showed up for lemonade and more Pam-and-the-twins-home-baked Greek Tea Cookies, which turned out to be a messy idea—powdered sugar and black tuxedos make for a bad combination. I think Kemi might have been hoping that, despite all of the legal battling, her mom would show up at our house with a camera to snap a few shots of her daughter going to her first prom, as Kemina had emailed her mother to fill her in on our pre-prom plans, but that didn't happen. In any case, I'm happy to share my family with her. I seem to have ended up with an extra mother.

So here we are, slow dancing barefoot to the soft sounds of a three-piece jazz band, under about a million white balloons, the glow of the white fairy lights that outline the doors and windows our only source of brightness. I think we both have that happy-and-sad-at-the-same-time senior thing going on in our heads—bittersweet memories coupled with plenty of exciting future hopes and dreams. I pull Kemi against me, and without the heels, I'm *almost* eye-to-eye with her. She bends her neck so that she can place her head sideways on my shoulder.

Before she gets too comfortable, I push her back a step; I've decided that right now is the moment I've waited for. Yes, it's the "perfect" time. Using American Sign Language, I make the sign for "I love you"—two fingers and my thumb pointing straight up in the way of concertgoers everywhere. Kemi looks at my oddly positioned fingers, and then into my eyes; her confused expression makes me happy I learned another way of expressing my sentiment. With three quick gestures—pointing to myself, crossing my arms in front of my chest, and then pointing to her—I again tell Kemina how I feel. This time she smiles widely and nods, and then pulls me back against her, saying softly, "I love you, too, Justine."

If that's not perfect, I don't know what is.

Mia Kerick is the mother of four exceptional children—all named after saints—and five nonpedigreed cats—most named after the next best thing to saints, Boston Red Sox players. Her husband of twenty-two years has been told by many that he has the patience of Job, but don't ask Mia about that, as it is a sensitive subject.

Mia focuses her stories on the emotional growth of troubled teens, young men, and their relationships, and she believes that sex has a place in a love story, but not until it is firmly established as a love story. As a teen, Mia filled spiral-bound notebooks with romantic tales of tortured heroes (most of whom happened to strongly resemble lead vocalists of 1980s big-hair bands) and stuffed them under her mattress for safekeeping. She is thankful to small presses and CreateSpace for providing her with an alternate place to stash her stories. Her only major regret: never having taken typing or computer class in school, destining her to a life consumed with two-fingered pecking and constant prayer to the Gods of Technology.

Mia has published works of adult contemporary gay romantic fiction with Dreamspinner Press and novels of contemporary LGBT YA fiction with Harmony Ink Press. Mia Kerick's books are recommended reads in the LGBT blogging/reading community, have spent many weeks on Amazon Hot New Releases and LGBT Best Sellers lists, as well as other notable bestseller lists, and have won awards for excellence in YA literature.

www.ingramcontent.com/pod-product-compliance
Lightning Source LLC
Chambersburg PA
CBHW061151170626
46809CB00003B/1046